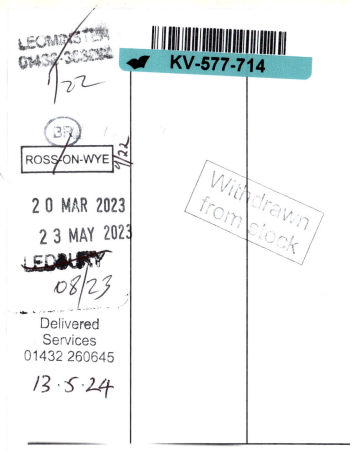

Please return/renew this item by the last date shown

**Herefordshire
Libraries**

**Herefordshire
Council**

PUPPY LOVE

When divorced mum-of-two Laurel decides to fill the gap in her family with a rescue dog, little does she know how much the Puppy Love Dog & Cat Sanctuary will change her life. Quite apart from gorgeous Labrador Alfie, there's the deeply attractive proprietor Jack . . . and his obsessive ex, Paula, who it seems isn't ready to release Jack from her claws any time soon!

DEBBIE CHASE

PUPPY LOVE

Complete and Unabridged

LINFORD
Leicester

First published in Great Britain in 2021

First Linford Edition
published 2021

A catalogue record for this book is available
from the British Library.

ISBN 978–1–4448–4803–8

Published by
Ulverscroft Limited
Anstey, Leicestershire

Printed and bound in Great Britain by
TJ Books Ltd., Padstow, Cornwall

This book is printed on acid-free paper

1

As soon as the search screen displayed itself on my computer, I quickly typed in 'local dog and cat sanctuaries'.

I wasn't sure why, but since Will and I split up and it was just me and my two children, Becky and Robbie, I had felt a longing for a pet. Either a sweet, fluffy cat or a cute dog — not a kitten or a puppy, but definitely an animal that had either been abandoned or ill-treated.

Bringing some happiness into the life of a sad animal was something I felt I needed to do at the moment. And then our family would be bigger again — not just the three of us but four, which, it seemed to me, was as it should be.

I scrolled through the list that had displayed itself. Cobby Cattery, Skelmanthorpe Sanctuary for Dogs and Cats, Arthur's Animals, Puppy Love Dog & Cat Sanctuary, Patty's Pooches, Cobby Animal Lost and Found . . . there were a lot of places to look at. However one in particular had caught my eye, and I scrolled back up to Puppy Love Dog & Cat Sanctuary.

There must surely be a story behind that name. I had a very strong memory of watching Donny Osmond on *Top Of The Pops* singing a song called *Puppy Love.* Surely the reason for the name wasn't that the proprietor had loved Donny as much as I had? I'd bought the record and played it, leaning dreamily over the turntable, thinking that there was no one in the world as wonderful as Donny Osmond.

Was this fate, then? Meant to be? Would I find what I was looking for there?

Puppy Love Dog & Cat Sanctuary, Bocking Lane, Hampthwaite. Brainchild of Jack Garthwaite.

'What are you looking at, Mum?' a voice in my ear made me jump and I turned around to see my daughter, Becky, peering over my shoulder.

At sixteen years old Becky looked

more like eighteen and wore skinny jeans teamed with a green top, her knobbly shoulders — covered in goose pimples — poking from the holes at the top of the sleeves. No wonder they were called 'cold shoulder' tops! Her shiny, dark hair fell in waves down her back and her pretty face was artfully made up with thick, black eyebrows and a slick of bright red lipstick.

I was just about to make a derogatory comment about wearing too much make-up for her age. Then I thought better of it as she said, 'Wow, you're looking at dog and cat sanctuaries? Are we going to get a dog?' She glanced at me. 'I bet you'd love one to run with, wouldn't you?'

'Well, yes, that would be great — but I was thinking more of an addition to the family. I feel we're a bit depleted at only three.'

'Yeah,' she muttered. 'You mean since Dad walked out on us.' She stalked off into the kitchen. Straight away I heard the soft purring of the kettle and the clinking of cups and spoons as she began to make herself a hot drink.

I followed her and stood in the kitchen doorway watching as she spooned coffee and sugar into a mug, then added milk and hot water.

Her whole body looked tense with hurt and I knew that even after almost a year, she was still suffering from the effects of what she considered to be her dad's betrayal. She'd put him on a pedestal and he'd fallen. Despite the fact that Will and I were on friendly terms, it looked very unlikely at the moment that like Lazarus, he would rise again to those heights of admiration.

'I'm sorry,' I said as I enveloped her in a hug feeling her body tight as a spring slowly relax and melt into mine. 'I shouldn't have made that comment. I'm very happy with the three of us, but the truth is, Becky, I'd love a pet around the house . . . a dog or a cat, it doesn't really matter. Would you?'

I felt a nod of her head against my shoulder so, feeling encouraged, I carried on.

'There's a place in Hampth-waite — it's called Puppy Love, would you believe? — which I've seen online. It isn't too far away, not far beyond Skelly. Do you fancy a trip out?'

She nodded again, then pulled away gently. She stood back against the work-top, picking up her drink and cradling it in both hands. Steam rose in a plume from the hot brew and the tantalising smell of coffee beans drifted around the room.

'Yeah, I think a dog would be good. I'd like to take a look . . . if we can get my little brother out of bed to come along, of course.'

She trailed out of the kitchen carrying her drink saying, 'I'll go and give him a shout . . .'

Satisfied that at the moment she was OK, especially as she wanted Robbie with us as well, I went back to my com-puter and made a note of the address of the Puppy Love Dog & Cat Sanctuary for the sat nav and also the name of the owner. I smiled to myself as I read again,

Brainchild of Jack Garthwaite.

I was curious as to what sort of man this Mr Garthwaite was. Most people would have simply said that they were the proprietor or the owner, not that the enterprise was their brainchild . . . hmm, definitely something different there!

Searching online again, I tried to find a website for the business so I could take a look at all the available cats and dogs before setting off. I couldn't find one and when I rang the telephone number, it went straight to voicemail. Maybe it was a very new business and wasn't up and running properly as yet.

Oh well, I thought. I'm sure I'll find out more when I get there.

I took a quick glance from the window before deciding whether or not to wear a jacket. It was only mid-September, yet already the leaves on the trees were beginning to turn breathtaking shades of red, orange and yellow and a deep crispy carpet had already laid itself as if by magic on the lawn. It was a fine day, though; the sky a deep blue with fluffy clouds freshly washed in Heaven's launderette floating amid the blinding lemon light of the sun.

I picked up a jacket just in case and when Becky and Robbie were ready, we trooped out to the car.

'Are we getting a dog, Mum?' asked Robbie as he settled himself in the back seat and Becky, as the eldest, folded herself into the front.

'We're just going to have a look,' I replied as I started up the engine and drove away from our house on the once much-maligned new housing development on White Church Lane and in the direction of Cobby village.

Yes, our new housing estate had been the subject of many newspaper articles since we'd moved in because, apparently, it was built on a green belt site and was also said to be on a flood plain. I was keeping my fingers crossed that no repercussions would arise because of this.

I glanced at Robbie in the mirror, at his cute face and snub freckly nose that

made him look younger than his thir-
teen years. He took after his dad with
his slight build and dark hair that just
scraped his shoulders.

'Can we get something ferocious like
a Pit Bull or a Rottweiler?' he asked in a
horror movie-type voice.

Becky turned in her seat and looked
at him scathingly.

'You're so stupid, Robbie. Those poor
dogs have bad reputations through no
fault of their own.'

I zoned out a bit as she gave Robbie a
good telling-off about his poor choice of
dog, but then catching sight of his woeful
face in the mirror I felt sorry for him and
wondered how the separation between
me and Will had really affected him.

I wasn't sure really, because he wasn't
as vocal and dramatic as Becky but kept
his feelings close to his chest. I worried
sometimes that he spent too much time
alone in his bedroom playing computer
games and even doing homework as if he
enjoyed it (should I really worry about
that?).

Then I reassured myself that he had friends — two in particular, Mark and Luke, local kids he hung about with. I knew that sometimes they played football in the park or rode their bikes to the river bank to fish — and a sudden interest in cricket was costing me a fortune with all the kit he said was vitally necessary.

He was also friendly with my brother's children, Ash and Willow, who lived nearby and often went round for a sleepover or to play computer games. My sister-in-law, Jane, was lovely. She had welcomed Robbie into her family as if he was her own son, as well as being a great support to me at the time of my break-up with Will.

'OK then,' I heard Robbie say. 'How about a spaniel or a Labrador? They're good dogs to have, aren't they? And they'd be good to run with Mum.'

'Ah, now you're talking,' said Becky. 'That's far more sensible . . . '

Robbie caught my eye in the mirror and gave me the thumbs-up sign. I grinned back and then laughed as I heard Becky say in her school teacher voice that if he kicked the back of her seat one more time, she'd make sure he never saw daylight again!

★ ★ ★

Cobby was busier than ever as it was a Saturday and the market, courtesy of Cobby Town Council, was in full swing.

I drove slowly past the hairdresser's, Cobby Cuts and Curls, where I worked part time as a senior stylist. Peering in through the window I saw two of my colleagues, Heather and Diane, and the manager, Jenny, doing all sorts of intricate things to their clients' hair.

I'd worked there for more than ten years now and since going part-time, had every other Saturday as one of my days off which I really enjoyed. Becky and Robbie gave the women little wiggly waves as we cruised by.

Just a bit further along the street was Bloomer's the Bakers where my new neighbour, Maggie Sears, used to work.

Well, she was Maggie Gates now since she had married Stephen, the headmaster at Cobby High School, where Becky used to go to and where Robbie went now.

Maggie worked at the school too and was involved in the exams, which was great as she had been a great support to Becky throughout. I'd always got on well with her even though, at fifty-four, she was seven years older than me.

Bloomers looked really busy as usual with a long queue trailing out of the door and almost into the pound shop opposite. I made a mental note of this and decided I would go there later when it was quieter, specifically for my fix of a Belgian bun (if there were any left of course)!

Leaving the town behind, we passed emerald fields full of creamy sheep, black and white cows and sleek horses that nibbled the grass and constantly shook their heads, their manes flying against thick clouds of circling black flies.

Skelmanthorpe soon appeared on our

left, the outskirts higgledy-piggledy now with the new housing estates that had sprung up like mushrooms in the once pretty green fields.

I'd been born in Skelmanthorpe, or Skelly as we always called it, and it was a shock every time I visited to see how much it had changed and how big it was getting, gradually growing wider and wider like someone with middle-aged spread. We could see the newly refurbished petrol station, the beautiful building that housed the gym and swimming pool called Hale & Hearty, and a small complex of shops together with a somewhat battered-looking pub called The Owl's Nest which led onto the main street and into the older part of the town with its narrow, twisty lanes.

The sat nav piped up telling me that I had a left turn coming up. Sure enough, a sign for Hampthwaite appeared and then there was a sudden right turn which took us down a country lane where trees arched overhead, creating a pretty, leafy, green tunnel.

The tiny village of Hampthwaite with its beautiful thatched cottages passed by in a blur until another sharp right took us up a very steep hill, so steep that even in second gear my little Citroen struggled along like a flagging marathon runner.

Thankfully the ground soon flattened out and a pair of open wooden entrance gates came into view. Next to them was a barely discernible sign, almost hidden by trailing ivy and painted a mucky orange, its writing faded, telling us in the exact same wording as online that we had arrived at Puppy Love Dog & Cat Sanctuary, Bocking Lane, Hampthwaite, brainchild of Jack Garthwaite.

All three of us jerked from side to side like puppets as I crunched the car over the unmade stony car park and after pulling into a space we sat and looked around at our glorious surroundings.

The sanctuary nestled on a hill amid striped golden fields, like a rather fine chocolate in a crinkly paper, its buildings open to the sun and the sky and the beautiful views all around. Leafy trees in an array of green and golden hues stood against the horizon, merging with strands of cobwebby clouds, and a skein of geese flew across the blue in a V formation. I'd visited the tiny village of Hampthwaite before but hadn't ventured much further, and had no idea that this place was here. What a find!

Getting out of the car, we walked further into the sanctuary where we could see large wire mesh-fronted sheds and outhouses, all with sturdy wooden doors with deep latches. Rough barking and high-pitched meows rang out through the hot, still air. A woman wearing a bright red dress, a small child hunkered down beside her, gazed avidly into one of the sheds. The child chuckled and tried to put her tiny fingers through the mesh to touch a snoozing cat curled in a tight black and white ball. A couple of young girls wearing green overalls, the words *Puppy Love Dog & Cat Sanctuary* in swirly yellow lettering across their bib fronts, swept the corridors between the outhouses while a young boy spooned cat and dog food into large silver bowls.

Becky, Robbie and I walked slowly from one outhouse to another looking at the mewling and growling furry bodies inside. I noticed that the dogs and cats were situated in separate areas and all came closer as we walked past, sniffing through the mesh and weighing us up as potential forever friends.

'Look at this one,' said Becky, pointing to a cute little Westie that rose up on its hind legs and scrabbled at the netting with its paws as we came nearer to its outhouse. She pointed to a sign attached to the mesh. 'She's called Nellie, and — '

'She wouldn't be any good for running,' said Robbie. 'Not with those little legs.'

A voice cut into our giggles at Robbie's remark and we all turned around to see who it was.

'Hi here guys, can I be of any help?'

A figure stood in front of us who at first glance I thought was perhaps the blueprint of a hero for the cover of a romantic novel. Well, he could do with a hair and beard trim (actually, quite an extensive trim), but shining out from among all that facial hair he had the most beautiful blue eyes framed by long black lashes. I was mesmerised by them. He wore an overall as the other workers did, but his seemed to emphasise his muscular physique more than any of the others.

I must have looked taken aback at his sudden appearance because he said, 'Jack Garthwaite at your service, madam,' and gave a deep bow with a wave of an arm like an old fashioned courtier.

'Oh, so all this is your brainchild,' I said, laughing and spreading my arms wide. I hoped he couldn't see how shocked I was that a man with his looks was here in a dog and cat sanctuary in Hampthwaite, and not lazing by a swimming pool in Hollywood or somewhere equally upmarket. 'Very pleased to meet you. I'm Laurel Masters and these,' pointing to my children, 'are my daughter, Becky, and my son, Robbie.'

'Pleased to meet you,' he said, bowing to Becky and Robbie and they — in bewilderment, it seemed — bowed back. 'Are you looking for a cat or a dog?'

'A dog,' piped up Robbie. 'A puppy . . . '

'Something cute,' put in Becky. 'Nothing ferocious.' She gave Robbie a sidelong glance.

'Um, no,' I butted in. 'Not a puppy — something a little older I think, maybe three or four?' I studiously ignored Robbie's pleading looks and concentrated instead on Jack Garthwaite whose appearance absolutely astounded me and certainly made my heart rev up a beat or two, something that hadn't happened for a long, long time. Now, if I could just get to work on that hair and beard.

'Hmm,' said Jack, cupping his mouth with his fingers and narrowing those baby-blues as he thought. 'OK, not a puppy, just a bit older and nothing ferocious . . . I may have the very dog. Follow me, guys.'

We stumbled across the stony car park in his wake, a tall, muscular figure, his stride long and easy, to another set

17

of outhouses. There with a flourish, he pointed out a little black dog that lay quietly alone, its long nose laid out on its paws. The dog seemed to be sleeping but must have sensed someone approaching as it rose to its feet then sat back on its haunches, looking at us through the mesh, its soft brown eyes apprehensive yet its tongue lolling from its mouth as if in a smile.

He wagged his tail furiously and gave a deep woof as I walked nearer, hoping — I suppose — that I had meaty treats hidden in the depths of my bag. All three of us leaned closer to read the little white plaque that was attached to the mesh,

Hello, I'm Alfie the Labrador. My owner, who I loved very much, died and left me all alone. I'm just a year old and in need of my fur-ever home, good long walks and runs, and plenty of TLC. If you'd like to be my friend, speak to Jack today.

'I put Alfie on his own for a while because he was a bit nervous when he first arrived,' pointed out Jack. 'The barking of the other dogs seemed to make him worse. His owner was an elderly lady who died suddenly at home and poor Alfie was left indoors with her for a couple of days and he was a little upset. Unfortunately her family — only one son, I hasten to add — couldn't take him and, well, here he is.'

'Hello, Alfie,' I said bending down, my nose almost touching the wire.

'Ah, how cute,' said Becky, as Alfie pressed his nose against the mesh to meet mine. 'Poor Alfie, being with his owner for so long after she'd died . . . '

My expression must have looked ambiguous because Robbie said, 'Yeah, and you did say you wanted a dog you could help, didn't you Mum? And I think Alfie needs help.' He hunkered down to Alfie's level and, poking a finger through the mesh, gently stroked the top of his head.

'Yes, I did,' I replied. 'But this dog is so young . . . I wanted an older dog.'

'I thought you wanted a dog to run with?' pressed Robbie.

'Yeah,' said Becky. 'And Labradors are great runners, aren't they?' she asked, looking at Jack.

'Oh, yes without a doubt,' Jack replied. 'They could run all day!'

'And all night?' asked Robbie.

'Oh you two, please,' I said. 'Stop confusing Mr Garthwaite. I just didn't want one quite so young, that's all.'

'Please call me Jack,' he said, and then pointed out, 'Well, there will be other dogs. You don't have to take the first one you see but the dogs I have at the moment are either tiny newborn puppies which you couldn't take just yet anyway, or dogs a lot older than Alfie . . . dogs of between seven and ten years old.

'I have a Westie, Nellie, who's eight, Minty, a Border Collie who's nine, oh and there's Rex, a German Shepherd. He's even older though, he's almost eleven . . . but you'd need to come back another day if you want a dog of, say, three or four years old. If you leave your contact details I could let you know when a dog of that age comes into the sanctuary,

20

but of course, the decision is yours.'

'Mum?' asked Robbie.

'Mum?' asked Becky.

Becky and Robbie and indeed Jack Garthwaite gazed at me in anticipation. I was aware of the rustling of the wind as it moved amongst the trees and the warmth of the sun on the top of my head, even the slightly fusty smell of the animals' cages registered in my mind as I stood and thought, gazing all the time at Alfie the little black Labrador. And before anyone dared to say another word, I knew that I'd come to a decision.

★ ★ ★

I trailed my finger down the list of clients for that day. Mrs Wilson was coming for a shampoo and set at nine o'clock, then Mrs Jowett at eleven o'clock for a cut and blow dry. I was pleased to see that Kath Timpson, Cobby Town Council's town clerk, was due in at one o'clock for her colour, trim and blow dry. It was always good to see Kath and how she'd

21

blossomed over the years after the sad death of her husband, Johnny Emmerson, a few years ago.

She'd been a regular client of mine for a long time now but I'd never forgotten the first time she'd come in, just after her husband died. She'd rung, desperate for a good haircut and almost in tears. Of course I'd fitted in her straight away and what a difference the cut had made, not only to her appearance but her self-esteem as well. Something as simple as a good haircut can be such a boost when you're feeling as down as she was.

Her life had changed now, though, and from what I could see she was very happy with her new husband, town planner Paul Timpson.

Thinking about makeovers, I was pretty sure that Jack Garthwaite from the Puppy Love Dog & Cat Sanctuary could benefit from one. He had outstanding eyes and I could just see him with shorter hair and a tidier beard. Wow! No man had appealed to me in such a way for years!

My phone beeped and glancing at it, I saw it was a text from Becky reminding me that I needed to go back to Puppy Love to get Alfie's treatment card. We'd left it behind when we'd taken him home with us the week before. Yes, OK, I know, I'm a sucker for big brown eyes and a lolling tongue — but only in a dog, of course! And I'm a sucker for a good running partner and, my goodness, he certainly lives up to that. He can outrun me any day.

The door suddenly pinged open and Mrs Wilson, my first appointment of the day, walked in, her face wreathed in a smile of happy anticipation. I held out my hand for her coat and led her to a chair for her much-awaited hour of relaxation. Then at another ping of the door I gave Jenny a shout as her first client of the day arrived — a young girl with a waterfall of dirty-blonde hair that reached her knees, who was asking for it all to go.

She looked slightly nervous as she took her seat, although apparently her words over the phone had been, 'I'm so sick of my hair — just cut it all off!'

Inhaling the lovely coconut aroma of the shampoo as I carefully massaged my finger-tips over Mrs Wilson's hair and scalp, her head lolling languidly from side to side, I made up my mind that as I finished work at two o'clock that day, I would visit the sanctuary to pick up Alfie's treatment card.

And also maybe, if he wasn't too busy, I would have a chat with the boss of the establishment and try to workout what was going on with Mr Hollywood, or the enigma that was Jack Garthwaite!

2

I knew a long time before it happened that my ex-husband, Will, and I would have to go our separate ways.

Neither of us had met anyone else; that definitely wasn't what had come between us. I think the problem was that we had just stopped loving each other. Not entirely — we were still fond of each other in a brother and sister kind of way — but the romance and the closeness that we'd shared after meeting at such a young age seemed to have disappeared into thin air.

We'd tried so hard to get it back, had spent hours having long, meaningful chats, but as Elvis used to say, *'A little less conversation, a little more action please!'* We'd tried that too and had made the effort to dress up and go out on date nights leading to various amorous scenes in the bedroom, but all to no avail. Neither of us even wanted to hold hands any more or had the desire for a peck on the cheek, let alone the lips, and cuddles were increasingly rare. So one day, after yet another strained talk, he packed his bags and moved out.

He'd already found a little flat in Cobby Village above the estate agents Bedrock & Rose, courtesy of Maggie Gates' sister, Lynette, who worked there and had mentioned that the flat above was coming up for let. He seemed to like it there on his own. It suited him. He could be as obsessively tidy and clean as he wanted to be and for computer nerd, Will Masters, that was an integral part of his life — like breathing.

Since he moved out we were often in touch and now had a cordial relationship. He spent time with Becky and Robbie — albeit, on Becky's part, a moody stalking around sort of time which I'm sure Will didn't understand at all at the moment. Whereas Robbie liked to play computer games with him and often asked for a rough and tumble game of football. I'm pretty sure Will opted for the sparseness and cleanliness of the computer games most of the time. That would be right up his street.

Thinking about it, though, I maybe wasn't as devastated as I should be at the break-up — just really sad. Sometimes, late at night after a glass or two of wine, I worried that we hadn't made enough of an effort to stay together. After all, almost twenty years of marriage was a big deal. Clear-headed the following day though, I knew that really we had tried very hard to make a go of it, and I was glad that he was still in my life and doing his best to be a good father to our children.

These thoughts were running through my mind as I left work that afternoon and made my way out to the car park. It had been a busy day and my hands were sore from their immersion in so much water, shampoo and conditioner. Not only had I had a few cuts-and-blow-dries but also a perm and a couple of colours, one of which was a lady who had gone from dark to very light all in one go. Although it looked good to me, it would be interesting to see next time whether she would revert to dark again. Some clients couldn't cope with such a dramatic change.

I drove slowly through Cobby Village giving a cheery wave out of the window to Kath Timpson as she walked along the High Street holding tightly to the arm of Paul Timpson and proudly showing off her new hairdo. It gave me a real boost when I saw clients out and about with freshly washed and gleaming hair that had been styled by me.

This brought to mind again Jack Garthwaite and how I would give anything to slice my scissors through his thick, dark hair. The thought of drugging his coffee and rendering him helpless had flitted through my mind, as I guessed that might be the only way I would be able to get close enough to him to do it. Which was a shame!

I spotted the left turn for Hampthwaite straight away (sorry, sat nav, but I don't need you any more) and then the sharp right where once again I drove down that lovely country lane with the trees arching overhead creating a long leafy tunnel. Sunlight fell in shimmering rods, illuminating the leaves making them shine bright green, red and orange. It dazzled my eyes so that, squinting, I had to pull down the car's visor to see properly.

After the climb up the massive hill, my poor little Citroen grinding its gears in despair, Puppy Love Cat & Dog Sanctuary's gates came into view flanked by its dilapidated old orange sign.

I pulled into the stony car park and sat in the car for a few minutes admiring the beautiful view that was spread out on all sides like a patchwork quilt, gazing at the varying shades of green and gold fields interspersed with the deep umber of higgledy-piggledy dry stone walls.

I couldn't help thinking how clever Jack Garthwaite had been to pick such a gorgeous location for his sanctuary. Not only was it a breath of fresh air for visitors, but a fabulous location for the animals to live until they were re-homed.

Walking away from the car, I could see a lot of people milling around the building that housed the office area, some carrying cat baskets, some with dogs on leads and bags full of treats, plastic litter trays and toys. Others held envelopes no doubt with their pet treatment cards inside and Puppy Love business cards that Jack gave out to people who adopted an animal. As I got closer I could see him moving about inside the office, typing information into the computer, printing off the certificates that people received for the adoption of a pet, and handing animals into their cages and carrying baskets.

I saw he had a young girl helper proudly wearing her volunteer badge stating that her name was Kayleigh and asking whether she could be of any assistance. She was doing her best but even so, it looked to me as if he needed a few more helpers, the place was so busy.

Just as that thought ran through my mind I noticed a small card stuck on the office door and peering closer, saw that

Puppy Love Dog & Cat Sanctuary was looking for a part time admin assistant, one or two days a week. *If you are interested, please have a word with Jack or send in your CV.*

Yes, I thought, *that's exactly what he needs*. I was surprised actually that he didn't already have an assistant. It was a big place and if he was managing with just a few volunteers then he was doing a sterling job.

On the spur of the moment I fumbled in my bag for my phone and took a picture of the advert. Just in case.

Yeah, just in case of what? I asked myself.

Oh you know . . . just in case, replied my little inner voice that knew no better!

As the amount of visitors thinned out and there were just a few people over by the outhouses admiring the cute animals, I poked my head around the office door. Jack was sitting at the computer looking at something on the screen, then running his finger down a printed list at his side. He looked smart and really cool, even though he wore just a pair of jeans and a shirt open at the neck showing a mat of chest hair that for some strange reason I didn't dare to look at so hurriedly averted my gaze.

I don't know why but I felt slightly self-conscious as I said, 'Oh, hi, I'm Laurel Masters . . . I adopted Alfie last week. The black Labrador.'

He turned straight away and, smiling, said, 'Oh yes, hello there. No doubt you've come for Alfie's treatment card? Sorry I forgot to remind you.'

I nodded as I glanced around noticing that the office, which was only very small, was in a state of total disarray. Papers were piled high on Jack's desk surrounding him like a barricade, open boxes of cat and dog treats and collars spilled over onto the floor and every available space seemed to be filled, including the walls which had old, wrinkled posters peeling off at the corners. Several old calendars dating back two or three years dangled from rusty nails.

Even though I tried to hide my expression, he must have noticed because he said, shamefaced, 'Sorry about the mess. I've been on my own with only a handful of volunteers for quite a few months now and it's difficult to keep track of everything. It can get very busy here . . . so busy,' he said, twitching at his beard with his fingers, 'It's been ages since I had time to go for a proper hair and beard cut! I must look like a wild man!'

He stood up, walked towards me and held out his hand, saying, 'It's good to meet you again, Mrs Masters.'

'Oh, please, call me Laurel,' I said as, surprisingly, a frisson of shock coursed through my body at the touch of his hand. His bright blue eyes shone out from his slightly unruly hair and beard, which for some strange reason made my heartbeat quicken until it was clattering away in there like a mad thing! What on earth was wrong with me?

Before I could say anything he continued, 'An unusual name.'

I smiled. 'Yes — my mum is a bit of a hippy and likes natural names of trees and bushes and even flowers for babies.'

I conjured up an image of my mum wearing a long flowing skirt, a headband around her cloud of curly hair, and lots of bracelets encircling her arms that jingled and jangled as she moved. I gabbled on, 'My brother is called Rowan and he has two children, Ash and Willow!'

'Fabulous,' he replied. 'What about your dad? Is he a bit of a hippy too?'

'Um, not really, he just goes along with my mum. I think he'd have been quite happy to call me Bert if she'd suggested it.'

Jack laughed long and loud and I noticed he had well-shaped lips in amongst the beard. I chided myself. *What is wrong with you, Laurel?*

My eyes were drawn again to the open necked shirt and the little slice of Jack's chest that I could see as he said, 'How's Alfie coming along? I hope you don't regret your decision to take him?'

Tearing my eyes away and looking straight into his blue eyes, I said, 'Oh, no, not at all. He's a lovely dog, so loyal and affectionate. And he's such a good running companion! All three of us are very happy with him.'

'Ah, yes, I suspected you were a runner . . . you've certainly got the figure for it.' At which point Jack seemed to get rather flustered before saying abruptly, 'Well, I mustn't keep you.' He rushed over to his desk and picked up a white envelope with *Mrs Laurel Masters* printed on it in thick black script. 'Here you are. Don't forget Alfie's treatment card this time.'

'Thank you,' I said, as he thrust the envelope into my outstretched hand — rather abruptly I thought. Still seeming rather flustered, he stood staring at me and just when I thought he was about to say something else, there was a tap at the office door. A young couple peered in, enquiring if he had any kittens for adoption at the moment.

Feeling very awkward and in the way now that Jack had some potential customers, I said goodbye and raising a hand to him, left the office. I crunched my way back over the car park, taking one last, lingering look at the animals as I walked past.

Sitting in the car, I could just about see Jack and the young couple making their way over to the outhouse where he kept the newborn kittens. He walked very quickly as if with great purpose, the couple trailing behind him deep in conversation about the colour, breed and possibly sex of their new moggie, I imagined.

Reluctantly I started up the car and began slowly and carefully to turn it around, certainly not one of my strong points, so that I could drive safely through the large wooden gates and back out onto the road which would take me home to Cobby. The admin job that I'd seen advertised on the office door stayed in my mind and I thought how lovely it would be to work with the animals for a day or two a week.

Whoever got the job would be a very lucky woman . . . or indeed man.

Gazing in the rear view mirror I saw that Jack had stopped at the door to let the young couple into the outhouse before him. As he did so, he turned and looked after me as I manoeuvred the car out of the gates. He waved, his hand moving like a little white flag. Lowering the window, I stuck my arm out and waved back, with thoughts tumbling through my mind — the main one being, for some inexplicable reason, would I ever see him again?

* * *

Alfie sat next to me as close as he could possibly get, his dark brown eyes flicking backwards and forwards and watching my every move. It felt weird to be under such close scrutiny while eating my breakfast cereal.

I shook my head at him as I said, 'Alfie, you wouldn't like this. It's cereal — not very appetising for a dog.'

'Woof,' he said, meaning I'm sure, 'Hooman, I'll eat anything . . . try me!'

It was a Saturday again and four weeks since we'd adopted Alfie, three weeks since I'd gone to the Puppy Love sanctuary to pick up his forgotten treatment card, and so three weeks since I'd seen the very enigmatic Jack Garthwaite.

I couldn't understand myself because, even with the beard that needed a trim, I still found something alluring about him. But then I'd always been a sucker for men with facial hair and big blue eyes. Will had looked a proper rocker with his long, messy hair when I'd first met him all those years ago.

I had been sorely tempted to apply for the admin job, as I was sure that I could fit in another day's work with my part-time hairdressing. Of course now that I was a single parent, an extra bit of income would be good — and what a lovely job it would be, working with the animals — but I hadn't sent my CV in and felt that now it was probably too late. I assumed that Jack would have found a super-efficient person who had already started the job and got everything under control.

Visions of a beautiful young blonde

woman flashed into my mind and I imagined Jack enduring a long-overdue hair cut just so that the two of them could get closer.

I frowned as I tried to guess at Jack's age. It was difficult to tell but I would say around mid-forties, maybe a little younger, or maybe a little older than me. There'd never been any mention of a woman in his life but then again we hadn't touched on that subject or anything relating to it, and I was still trying to work out why he'd got so embarrassed when we'd talked about me being a runner. Maybe it was because he'd mentioned my figure? Did he like my figure?

I shook my head at my silliness and told myself to forget about him. Why should I be interested in a man who looked like a Hollywood heart-throb anyway? I'd always thought that men who were too good-looking couldn't be trusted! What had my mum always said? *Good looks attract the eyes, personality attracts the heart.*

I stood up and, putting my empty

bowl in the dishwasher, peered from the kitchen window. It was a fine sunny day, the sky a bright blue with just a few straggly clouds marring its surface. The lilac tree, its beautiful aromatic flowers dry and brown now, bent and swayed energetically in the strengthening breeze. This was a good sign as it wouldn't be too warm for a run, which was exactly what I had planned for myself and Alfie this morning. I knew for sure that Alfie, the fastest runner in the world, would have no objections to that.

I was just about to go upstairs to get changed, Alfie following closely on my heels as if he knew where I was going and what I was going to do, when Robbie stumbled into the kitchen wearing a pair of creased pyjamas, rubbing his eyes and yawning so hard that his open mouth was a deep black cavern in his face.

'Hi Mum . . . hello, Alfie.' He bent down to the dog's height and, throwing his arms around him, pulled him close and kissed the top of his head. I noticed that Alfie snuggled into his shoulder and when Robbie pulled back, heartily licked his face with his long pink tongue.

'Hi Robbie, are you OK?' I asked as he pulled himself wearily to his feet and went to the cupboard to get a bowl and a box of cereal, then opened the fridge door for the milk.

'Yeah ... if I could get some sleep ... if Becky wouldn't keep talking all night ... yap, yap, yap.' He made an opening and closing motion with his fingers and thumb.

I frowned as I said, 'Talking all night? Are you sure?'

'Yeah, course I'm sure,' he said irritably, then looked straight at me, while chewing cereal, his mouth going round and round like a cement mixer, 'Sounds pretty lovey-dovey too ... she must have an online boyfriend or something.'

'What do you mean, lovey-dovey?' I asked, feeling slightly panicked. 'What was she saying?'

'Well, you know ...' He spooned cereal so quickly into his mouth that beads of milk spluttered down his chin

as he spoke in a high pitched woman-
ish voice, '*Oh darling . . . do you love me?*'
then made a kissing sound with his lips,
'*Mou, mou, mou . . .* ' As he grinned up at
me, his dark eyes danced with mischief.

I smiled wryly and said, 'You had me
worried there, Robbie — story-teller.'

'No, it's true, Mum! Ask her. She's
being all lovey-dovey with someone.
Trust me.'

I looked at him, narrowing my eyes,
weighing him up so to speak, then said,
'I'm going upstairs to get changed. Alfie
and I are going for a run — do you fancy
it?'

Robbie had been known to accom-
pany us on a run every now and then.

'Nah, thanks Mum, but I'm going
round to see Ash. He's got the new
Bright Galaxies computer game — it's
the second in the trilogy and supposed
to be really good, even better than the
first, and he's asked me to have a game
with him. Then I'm meeting Mark and
Luke for a bike ride.'

Smiling at his enthusiasm, I went

upstairs, Alfie hot on my heels, and changed into running gear of black leggings and a black long-sleeved top over which I wore a bright green running vest. On the way back downstairs and thinking of what Robbie had just told me, I loitered on the landing and, pressing my ear against Becky's bedroom door, listened carefully just in case she was having a so-called lovey dovey conversation with an unknown person. But all was quiet now so I guessed she was still asleep — more than likely if she had been awake all night!

As I was about to turn away, I heard a lot of high pitched giggles then Becky's voice saying, 'Yes, it would be great if we could meet up out of college. We never see each other out of college . . . ' Then more giggles, and then another silence.

Such a long silence this time that I was just about to take my ear away from the door when she said, making me jump, 'When?'

Silence, more giggles, then, 'OK, if you can't make it any earlier, next

Saturday then, around six o'clock . . . '

The rest was unintelligible interspersed with a lot of laughter, so I couldn't catch where they were going to meet, or indeed who she was going to meet. What should I do?

Hmm . . . maybe I should have a word with her about this before jumping to conclusions.

Without further ado I pressed down on the handle, opened Becky's bedroom door just a tiny bit and peered in.

She started when she saw me and said, 'Hi Mum . . . you OK?' before clicking her mobile off and putting it on the bedside cabinet.

'Yeah.' I indicated towards the bed. 'May I?'

She nodded her head so I turned back to Alfie and, pointing my finger at him said, 'Stay.' He stared at me, his face mournful and sad as if to say, *I thought we were going for a run!*

Going into Becky's room, I closed the door and sat down on the edge of the bed.

'What's going on, Becky? Who have you been talking to for half the night?'

'No one!' She frowned and crossed her arms over her chest looking uncannily like the five-year-old she used to be.

'Oh, come on. Robbie heard you last night and I heard you just now, arranging to meet someone.'

The only reply was a stony silence so I persisted, 'Come on, Becky, this is important. What's going on?'

'Robbie's snitched on me!' She sat back against the headboard and literally pouted.

'If you don't want anyone to hear, then maybe you should speak a little more softly? You'll have to tell me, Becky — otherwise no phone, no laptop, no going out for a whole week!'

'Oh Mum,' she exclaimed really annoyed. Then she suddenly blurted out, 'Fine. I've got a boyfriend!'

'Wow! That's great, Becky. Why does that have to be a secret?'

She shrugged. 'I didn't think you'd approve!'

'Well . . . who is he?'

'Tom Blatchford,' she said faintly.

'Ah,' I replied, knowing now why she didn't want me to know. The Blatchford family were well known in our area and the eldest son, Danny, had recently spent a few nights in prison for petty thieving and goodness knows what else.

'I see . . .'

'He's nothing like his brother, Mum,' she cried passionately. 'Tom doesn't approve of him and wants to leave home as soon as he can, but he's only seventeen. Please don't tell me I can't see him . . .'

Tears were running down her pretty face.

'Hey,' I said. 'Don't cry, Becky, everything will be OK.' With serious misgivings I pulled her to me and gently stroked her hair as she wept, wondering what on earth would be the outcome of this.

Whatever the result, though, who was I to judge? I certainly wouldn't think badly of Tom just because of what his brother had done. What was that saying?

It is better to risk saving a guilty man, than to condemn an innocent one! Hmm, something like that. In any case, I'd always stand by Becky whatever she wanted to do and I'm sure that she was aware of that.

'Hey, don't cry, Becky. Look, I heard you making arrangements for Saturday at six o'clock?'

She lifted her eyes, nodded and sniffed. 'Where do you usually meet?'

'In the park.'

'Well, bring him here instead. I'll make something nice for tea.'

'Really?' She dabbed at her tears with a fingertip, until, digging in my pocket I found a pack of tissues and handed her one.

'Yes, really . . . call me nosey but I want to meet him anyway.'

'I've told him all about you and Robbie. And Alfie.'

'Well, he should definitely come and meet us then. Saturday at six . . . make it a date!'

She smiled and said, 'I'll message him

tonight. He'll be so pleased, Mum, I know he will.'

I gave her a reassuring hug while crossing my fingers in the hope that everything would turn out.

3

I'd spent ages looking at the screen of my computer, my fingers hovering uncertainly over the keyboard. Should I send it or should I not?

I'd spent a while checking and re-checking my CV and now it really was good to go, but my fingers just wouldn't do what they were supposed to do and press the send button!

Alfie lay at my side snoozing, his furry body moving up and down like a pair of bellows as he breathed and his floppy ears twitching as he dreamed. He certainly didn't seem bothered about whether or not I sent the CV to Jack Garthwaite.

Then all of a sudden, before I even knew what I was doing, I pressed the button and whoosh, it was gone! Where it would be now? Milling around somewhere in the ether, or maybe already sitting patiently in Jack's inbox waiting for him to read it? I had a feeling that I was too late in sending it but, hey, it was worth a try, especially as it was a job I would really like to do. I looked in my sent items folder. I could see it sitting there, so yes, it had definitely gone . . . now I would just have to wait and see what happened.

Raising my arms above my head, I gave myself a good stretch and then gently rolled my head from side to side to ease the stiffness in my neck. Glancing at my watch I saw that it was almost lunchtime. Bloomers the bakers beckoned. I could almost taste a tuna baguette followed by one of their Belgian buns — hmm, maybe I could incorporate that into a walk with Alfie — and as the weather was still sunny for the time of year we could have a picnic in the seated area by the Cenotaph. There was only the pair of us to worry about today as Robbie was at school and Becky, now that she'd finished her exams at college, was at a lecture about universities and her future studies. Unless of course, she opted to get a job and not go to university at all.

It didn't take much to wake the snoozing black Labrador.

'Walkies, Alfie, come on, boy.'

He sprang to his feet, tongue lolling from his mouth. Excited, he gave a few sharp woofs, so, attaching his brand new purple harness, we set off walking briskly into the village.

Cobby was crowded as it was such a glorious day and several people waved at me, some even crossing the road so they could get a good look at Alfie, exclaiming about what a gorgeous dog he was. Alfie wriggled his silky body beneath their patting hands, his tail wagging energetically.

Passing Bedrock & Rose, I stopped and glanced up at the windows of the little flat above to see if Will was there. The doors to the balcony were wide open, so he must be. I stared up, thinking that it would be good to see him and have a chat. I could tell him about Becky's boyfriend, sort of give him the heads-up.

I saw that he'd put out three earthenware pots which were full of blooms, the pinks, reds and yellows really brightening up the street.

Just as I was about to ring the bell on his smartly painted front door, he came out onto the balcony. He was sipping from a mug which I recognised as the 'Best Dad in the World' mug that Becky and Robbie had bought him for the last birthday he'd celebrated while living with us at home. I felt a wave of nostalgia wash over my heart.

'Hey,' I said, waving up at him. 'How are you?'

'Laurel.' A smile lit up his face which usually looked really serious and worried. I remembered him saying once after being asked if he was OK that yes, he was, and not to worry as this was just his normal expression. 'I'm fine. Where are you going?'

'I'm taking Alfie for a walk. I'm going to get a picnic from Bloomers and eat it on a bench by the Cenotaph. Do you fancy joining us?'

'Alfie?' he questioned, peering so far over the balcony that I was afraid he would fall and land splat at my feet!

Yuck! And then how would I be able to tell him about Becky's boyfriend?

'Our dog.'

'Good God,' he said. 'Of course, the famous Alfie. Two minutes . . . I'm coming down.'

In two minutes as promised he appeared outside, as breathless as if he'd run a mile, and pulling a jacket over his pale blue short-sleeved shirt. His brown hair, thinning on top now, was slightly too long but he was clean shaven, although rather thin and pale. Even in the warmest of weather, Will wasn't one for sunning himself. Alfie, straining at his lead, tried to get close, a smile of happy anticipation on his doggy face.

'Oh, whoa, whoa,' said Will holding up his hands palms forward.

'It's OK, he won't hurt you. He's just excited, that's all.'

'Yeah, I know. He's lovely, Laurel, but you know, I'm not used to dogs. But Robbie and Becky have told me all about him . . . '

'Yeah I thought they would have.

He's great, he makes a fabulous running partner.'

Will nodded as he strolled along beside me, dodging in and out of people coming the other way, young girls with pushchairs that they seemed to be using as battering rams, grizzling young kids, elderly people walking at a snail's pace.

'I'm glad you're here, I didn't expect you to be. What are you doing at home today?'

'Oh, I had a bit of time owing so decided to take a sneaky day off.' Looking sideways at me he grinned and I grinned back, glad that we were together, walking along in the sunshine, smiling at one another. Glad that we were still friends for the sake of Becky and Robbie, and all that we had been in the past.

Frowning now, he said, 'I'm glad I've seen you, Laurel — I've got something I want to talk to you about.'

'Oh, sounds ominous,' I said, puzzled.

'I'll tell you when we're settled on our bench.'

After a quick visit to Bloomers, Will

standing outside holding on self-consciously to Alfie's lead, we found a bench close to the imposing structure of the Cenotaph and sat down, putting our picnic in its paper bag beside us. There were a couple of men from the council working on the gardens around the Cenotaph, digging and weeding and planting bulbs. Alfie stretched out at our feet as we unwrapped our sandwiches and began to eat, my yearning for a Bloomers tuna baguette being more satisfied with every bite.

After a while Alfie sat up on his haunches. He sniffed the air and detecting food, watched us closely, his dark eyes shifting from one to the other as if he was watching a tennis match. I gave him a couple of his favourite treats, which he swallowed down happily enough, yet all the time keeping one vigilant eye on the treats and the other on us.

Nearly all the benches were full as people had opted to sit in the sunshine to eat their lunch and not hunched over their desk in a fluorescently lit office.

Pigeons fluttered and stalked, desperate for stray crumbs and Alfie gave one of the birds a very strange look when it flew over his head.

'This is pleasant,' said Will as he bit into his sandwich

'Yes. OK, fire away then.' I smiled at him.

He swallowed his food and then said, 'Well — to tell you the honest truth, Laurel . . . '

'Wait, I said. 'I know what you're going to say!' I faced him fully. 'You've met someone, haven't you?'

He looked at me and smiled wryly.

'Wow, that was quick. But then you always did know me so well.'

I didn't know what to say. I knew that this moment would come at some point — for either him or me, I suppose — and as much as I didn't want to get back with Will, it still hurt.

'Laurel?'

'That's um, that's great, Will. Who is she?'

'Her name's Liz, Liz Fletcher, and she

works at Cobby High School. She's an English teacher. Hey, maybe Becky and Robbie know her or know of her?' He glanced at me. 'But then again she's only been teaching there for around a year so maybe not.'

'Hmm,' I replied. 'Maybe Robbie does. Well, I'm glad for you, Will. I hope you and Liz will be happy together.'

He gave me another glance and a smile.

'Thank you, Laurel — ' He seemed to want to say something else but I interrupted.

'Becky has a boyfriend,' I blurted out, and before Will could speak, 'His name's Tom Blatchford.'

'Hmm . . . is he the brother of Danny?' I nodded, a wry twist to my mouth.

'Well, there's no cause for alarm as yet,' soothed Will. 'It doesn't mean he'll turn out like his brother . . . and Danny's young, he's a lot to learn. Kids are sometimes trouble when they're young. We were always getting a telling-off from the police.'

'Yes,' I said. 'But only for minor things.'

'Oh yes,' he said with a grin.

'I haven't met Tom yet,' I told him. 'I've invited him round this weekend.'

Will looked at me with an approving smile.

'That's great . . . you can help to keep them on the straight and narrow.'

'I don't really think I need to keep Becky on the straight and narrow, Will!'

'No, but good on you for taking an interest in her boyfriend however much you have reservations about him at the moment because of his brother. Becky will probably guess how you feel because of that connection.'

I sat inwardly digesting all this.

'Yes, she was very reluctant to tell me who he is, but I've set her mind at rest with my willingness to meet him.'

I raised my face to the sun. It was hot, burning my cheeks, sinking into my skin and giving me strength.

There was a short silence when suddenly he said, 'Has she forgiven me yet, Laurel?'

'Forgiven you?' I asked. 'Becky?'

'Yes. You know what I mean ... for leaving. Sometimes she's so cold with me.'

'She doesn't understand, Will. Don't forget she's only sixteen ... one day things will become clearer to her. Anyway, it wasn't just your decision, it was mine as well. I think that in the long run she'll realise that we're happier as we are now than if we'd stayed together.'

He didn't reply but just stared at me, his eyes becoming unfocused and vacant so that I could almost feel his brain whirring with thoughts.

I shivered as the air seemed to have gone a little colder and, glancing up, noticed that the clouds had begun to mass together like one big fluffy pillow, almost covering the lovely blue of the sky. Most of them were black-edged, swollen and looking fit to burst.

'I know,' said Will, following my gaze, disappointment evident in his voice. 'It looks as if it's going to rain.'

We began to pack up our picnic as the first drops fell and tugging gently at Alfie's lead, we hurried away, Will still clutching his coffee cup and turning up the collar of his jacket as we went.

Other people, idly enjoying the sunshine just as we had been, followed suit and as if in a mass walkout, the area around the Cenotaph suddenly emptied. The rain drummed down, soaking into the dry grass and the flower beds. The only people left were the two men from the council who carried on with their digging and planting as if it wasn't raining at all.

Will asked me to keep in touch and let me know when I'd met 'the boyfriend' as Bedrock & Rose and his flat came into view, the leafy green foliage hanging down from the balcony.

'Look, Laurel, just because I've met Liz, nothing will change. I'll always be there, for Becky and for Robbie too. Maybe one day she'll forgive me and we can get back to how we used to be.' He stood with his hands in his pockets and his shoulders hunched, streaky wet hair dangling in his eyes.

'She loves you, Will, but as I said earlier I think it will take a while for her to understand.' I shivered, hunching my shoulders almost to my ears, as Will leaned forward and pecked me on the cheek.

'Enough of that for now,' he said softly. 'You get home, you're freezing.'

Alfie barked softly as we began to hurry away through the glittering rain drenched streets.

I don't know why but I stopped and turned around to wave and saw that Will was still standing outside on the pavement. But there was a woman with him now, a woman of average height wearing well-cut jeans and a smart jacket. She had shiny, dark hair with a fringe that dangled into her eyes.

I heard Will say as he glanced at his watch, 'Liz! You're early. Good to see you . . . ' I couldn't hear what she said but she slid her arm around Will's waist as he fumbled in his pockets for the door key.

They disappeared then, swallowed up into the hole that was the doorway but it stayed with me, that action, the way the woman, Liz, had slid her arm possessively around Will's waist. And despite knowing that it was time for both of us to move on, it still made me feel incredibly sad.

★ ★ ★

I was fitting in a quick break in the staff room at Cobby Cuts and Curls while Mrs Leeming's dye was doing its work on her grey roots. I could see her reading a magazine and drinking tea, her hair piled up on top of her head and secured with a plastic clip.

An email suddenly popped up on my phone. Squinting — I always forget my reading glasses when I come to work — I could just about see that it was from Jack Garthwaite. With a growing sense of excitement, I clicked on it and using finger and thumb to make the text bigger, avidly read what it said.

Dear Mrs Masters (Laurel)
Thank you for sending your CV in application for the Admin Assistant job here at Puppy Love Dog & Cat Sanctuary. I'm

sorry for the delay in getting back to you.

Please could you come in for an interview next week? Would Wednesday at around 1pm be OK for you?

Regards
Jack Garthwaite

Yes, I thought. *An interview . . . brilliant . . . and Wednesday is just right as that's one of my days off!*

I rattled him off a quick reply — might as well do it straight away — saying, *Thank you for your email regarding my application for the Admin Assistant post. Yes, Wednesday at 1pm is fine for me. I look forward to seeing you then.*

Laurel Masters

I pressed the send button and putting my phone safely back in my bag went back into the salon to see how Mrs Leeming's roots were faring, feeling excited now at the thought of the impending interview. But, for some strange reason, I was feeling just a touch nervous at the thought of the up and coming visit from Becky's boyfriend, Tom Blatchford.

4

I sat in the car admiring the beautiful view yet again at Puppy Love Dog & Cat Sanctuary, just a little nervous about the interview but confident all the same.

I was sure I was just as strong as most people on my computer skills as well as having plenty of experience of dealing with the general public. After all I come across all sorts of different people working as a hairdresser — just as I'm sure most people do whether working in a hair salon, a shop, an office, or indeed an animal sanctuary.

It was a beautiful morning, overcast at the moment, but there was a hazy lemon sunshine trying its hardest to break through the clouds. I was glad that it was my day off as once the interview was over I'd decided that I'd go for a run with Alfie. I already had a route planned, an off-road route, that would take us through Cobby Village, along by the canal and then over the Glen towards Skelly . . . and then back home along the river bank. That would make a good run of at least six miles. Enough for me . . . but was it enough for Alfie, the ace running dog?

I'd spent ages that morning deciding what to wear for the interview and had opted for a plain outfit of a black trouser suit teamed with a white blouse. I wore minimal jewellery of silver hoops in my ears and one ring, a silver band on the ring finger of my right hand, a ring that I'd bought years ago with my very first salary while working as a legal secretary.

Jack, dressed in the overall that showed all his muscles so perfectly, was busy dealing with two customers who were evidently adopting a tiny Beagle puppy. He acknowledged my arrival with a wave of his hand as I peered into the office.

I noticed that the whole area looked marginally tidier than it had before and smiled at the thought of Jack making such an effort for his interviewees. 'Ah, Mrs Masters, Laurel, please take a seat.'

He indicated his own chair at the computer. 'I won't be two minutes . . . '

I glanced around but couldn't see another chair so wondered if Jack was going to interview me standing up!

I could hear him talking to the elderly couple who were adopting the puppy, and his positive comments when they told him that the puppy wasn't actually for them, but a birthday present for their granddaughter. I pictured him helping them put the puppy gently into its carrying cage and then giving them an envelope containing no doubt their adoption papers, treatment card and not forgetting the Puppy Love business card.

As I sat there, waiting, staring from the window at the beautiful view, a sudden image crossed my mind again of Will and the woman, Liz, standing on the pavement outside Bedrock & Rose. Her casual arm around Will's waist had reminded me of when Will and I had first met. Bringing back memories that I really didn't want to have — silly to think of them now, really. After all, we'd split up a long time ago and Will deserved happiness with a woman by his side, so things were turning out just as they should.

Jack's voice cut into my thoughts and I looked up in confusion.

'Sorry about the wait, Mrs Masters, um, Laurel . . . I had to find my helper, Kayleigh, she's looking after things for me while I interview you.'

He carried a sturdy wooden chair which he placed opposite me, and sat down heavily on it as if he was weary.

'Are you OK?' he asked, perhaps noticing my befuddled expression. 'Would you like a drink . . . a coffee or a glass of water?'

I don't know why but my throat felt as dry and rough as sandpaper.

'Um, yes please, a glass of water would be good.'

As he passed me a glass, which I sipped gratefully, he asked after Alfie. I told him he was fine and that I was planning a run with him that very afternoon. We then settled down to the interview and he asked me several questions about my computer skills, what jobs I'd had over the years, obviously trying to gauge my dealings with people and how I was at working with others or alone.

Once again my heart began to beat rapidly in my chest as his very blue eyes met mine, even noticing that when he smiled very fine wrinkles formed at each corner. As I'd thought before, if it wasn't for the slightly long beard, I had no doubt that he could look even more attractive. If only I had my scissors with me!

Bringing my thoughts back to the interview, I explained that most of my jobs since leaving college at seventeen had been office-based but then in my thirties, I'd decided to re-train as a hairdresser. For the most part I really enjoyed it but felt that an admin job would keep me up to speed with office work, which at times I missed — and, of course, here at the sanctuary there was the added bonus of working with the animals.

I pointed out that I would be more than happy to attend any training in animal behaviour that would help in my work with the dogs and cats. Jack assured me that he thought training was a brilliant idea and that he, as the company, would be able to fund any courses that I wished to do.

'How are you at setting up websites?' he asked. 'I desperately need a decent website with background information about Puppy Love and pictures of the animals and information about them too.'

'That would be no problem,' I assured him, 'I can set up a website and if it helps, a few years ago I did an online photography course so I'm not too bad at taking a picture or two either.'

We fell silent then, staring at each other, Jack weighing me up, so to speak.

Taking a deep breath, he said, 'OK then . . . Laurel . . . that was a good interview.' And leaning closer towards me he said softly, 'So when can you start?'

Thinking I was hearing things I said, 'What? Have I got the job? Have you no one else to interview?'

Jack smiled. 'Have you got the job? . . . yes, and have I anybody else to interview? . . . no. You are the last person on my list.' He flourished a piece of paper. 'And I like you best so I'm offering you the job.' Then he added, more professionally, 'I think you'll fit in really well here.'

'Thank you so much! I'm delighted. I accept.'

'One day a week to start off with?' Jack asked.

'Perfect!' I replied.

We shook hands, Jack assuring me that he would draw up a contract and email it as soon as possible. Outside, Kayleigh was chatting with a group of people who were staring in what seemed like rapture at a black and white kitten she was cradling in her arms.

I walked away, thoughts of the new job jostling through my mind. I heard Jack calling. Turning, I saw him hurrying over the stony car park.

'Laurel . . . We didn't arrange which day each week.'

Thinking of my hours at the hairdresser and mulling over which day would be best, I blurted out, 'Fridays?'

'Fridays are great,' he replied. He smiled broadly, his lips clearly visible in amongst his beard sending a shiver running down my spine.

He held out his hand again and with one last lingering look we parted. I got into my car and, manoeuvring carefully from the car park, made my way home.

★ ★ ★

'What on earth is that, Robbie?' I asked, noticing a large yellow and blue bruise on the top of his arm just barely covered by the sleeve of his T-shirt. We were having a lunchtime sandwich, the kettle bubbling away in the background along with the clinking of spoons and the rattle of plates. The view from the kitchen window was grey and discouraging and spits and spots of rain pattered against the glass.

He looked down sideways, peering

at the bruise, and then said, 'Oh, I was messing about with Ash . . . it's nothing, Mum.'

'Hmm,' I said. 'It doesn't look like nothing to me.'

'It looks like a massive yellow and blue bruise to me,' said Becky sarcastically from her seat at the kitchen table. She bit into a sandwich, her teeth very white against the brown of the bread, which was bursting at the seams with hunks of cheese and what looked like a whole jar of Branston pickle.

'Thought you were on a diet?' retorted Robbie, eyeing the sandwich and making a silly face.

'Drop dead, Robbie.' Becky was always very sensitive when it came to food and diets, although thank God, she didn't seem to deprive herself when she was really hungry! Alfie sat closely at her feet, watching her every move and hoping, no doubt, for a stray piece of cheese or even a pickle to fall to the floor.

'Stop it, you two,' I said sternly. 'And be quiet, Becky, that's an awful thing to say.'

To distract me I suppose, Robbie, energetically buttering bread at the worktop, said, 'So you're going to be working at the cat and dog sanctuary then, Mum?'

'Yes,' I said. 'How lucky am I?'

'What about the hairdressing?' asked Becky through a mouthful of sandwich.

'Oh, I'll still do that. Tuesday, Thursday and every other Saturday at the hairdresser, and Friday at the sanctuary.'

'Wow . . . did the Hollywood man interview you?'

I smiled wryly, wishing that I'd never said anything about Jack being as good-looking as a hero in a romantic blockbuster.

'I bet you'd love to get your scissors into his beard, wouldn't you, Mum,' Becky said knowingly.

Looking at my daughter, I noticed again that she was wearing far too much make-up for her age. Her eyebrows were too thick and black and her lips too red. What was she thinking?

I was so tempted to tell her that she looked ridiculous but clamped my mouth shut yet again. She was such a pretty girl even without any make-up, but I didn't want to dent her confidence by telling her what I really thought. Hopefully she would grow out of it and revert to a more natural look.

Thinking about it, though, I suppose I'd looked a lot like Becky when I was that age, minus the thick make-up of course. Although nowadays there seemed to be more and more grey streaks appearing in my dark hair that I could certainly do without. Perhaps I should ask one of the girls at the salon to cover them up for me or put in a few highlights. What did they say about getting lighter as you get older?

Sitting down at the table with my own meagre-looking salmon and cucumber sandwich and a steaming cup of coffee, I said, 'Yes, I would love to cut Jack's hair. Only a smidgen though, it would make all the difference.'

Alfie scooted close to me now, his attention diverted away from Becky by the enticing smell of the salmon.

'Hmm,' said Becky. 'Maybe if you did, the new Jack would like to take you on a date . . .'

I kept my face averted as I felt myself blushing poppy-red, and instead concentrated hard on Robbie as he too sat down at the table with a sandwich that looked even more substantial than Becky's!

'Oh, no,' I replied as calmly as I could. 'I don't think that would ever happen. I'm pretty sure that Jack will have a wife . . . and perhaps children of his own.'

'I think,' announced Becky, as she finished the last of her sandwich and, standing up, put her plate tidily in the dishwasher and then tore off a piece of kitchen roll to wipe her hands, 'that if Jack had a wife, there would be some evidence of it by now. After all you've had an interview with him. Wouldn't he have said something about her then?'

'Not necessarily,' I said. 'Why should he tell me about his private life?'

She shrugged and then giggled and just as the younger Becky would do, she put her arms around my neck and gave me a hug.

'I'm only teasing, Mum. I've got to go; I'm going round to Mandy's.'

As she sashayed out of the room, Robbie shook his head like an old man and said, 'See what I mean, Mum, she's acting strange, isn't she? Yap, yap, yap all night again.'

'Don't worry, Robbie,' I said, 'All has been revealed. You sister has got herself a boyfriend!'

'Wow, no way,' said Robbie, shaking his head.

'Who is it?'

'Somebody called Tom who she met at college!'

Robbie didn't really know much about the Blatchford family so I saw no reason at the moment to enlighten him.

'Wow, a boyfriend,' he said in wonder. 'So she's been talking to him during the night?'

'Yes it seems so,' I told him. 'But no doubt that will calm down in time. He's coming for tea on Saturday so you'll be able to meet him. Anyway, tell me more about that bruise on your arm.'

'I've told you, Mum, it's nothing. I was messing about with Ash and I fell.'

'Robbie, come on, you can tell me. Did someone hit you?'

'Mum . . .' As if on cue, his phone rang, buzzing and moving on the table beside him. Picking it up, he sidled from the room.

'Hey Ash, yeah . . . OK, I'll be round in ten.'

'Well . . .' I looked down at Alfie who was still sitting patiently at my side, his eyes huge, waiting no doubt for flakes of salmon to drop magically onto the floor. 'It's just you and me then, boy. Do you fancy a walk in the rain?'

'Woof,' he replied, still gazing at my plate.

Sighing heavily and wondering if I had another problem now, not just Becky but Robbie as well, I put the leftover salmon in Alfie's bowl and watched him wolf it down.

All sorts of worries were rushing through my mind and because of the bruises on Robbie's arm, I thought I'd give Rowan a ring to see if he could shed any light on it.

Picking up my mobile, I scrolled down to Rowan and pressed the button to ring. He picked up straight away.

'Hey Rowan, it's Laurel.'

'Hi Laurel, how's things?'

'All good, but I'm a bit worried about Robbie.'

'Why? He's coming round tonight, isn't he? Ash is raving about a new computer game they're going to play.'

'Oh yeah, I know but he's got these awful bruises on his arm and . . .'

'Oh, that'll be where he fell against the sideboard the other night. He was so excited at having won that computer game . . . um, what's it called, oh yes, Bright Stars, and they were having a bit of a play fight. You know what boys are like. I was meaning to ring because I know what a worrier you are!'

I laughed, my heart feeling lighter.

'Oh, brilliant. I've been quizzing him about them I'm afraid, I thought he was being bullied!'

'No . . . not at all,' replied Rowan. 'There's no need for you to worry about Robbie, Laurel. He's a good kid.'

'How are Jane and Willow?'

'Yeah, fine . . . all good here.'

'We must get together soon, OK?'

'Yeah, maybe a weekend? When we get a sunny day, we could all go for a walk.'

We decided that yes, a family walk would be on the cards very soon and I hung up with a feeling of relief, so glad that I'd rung and found out about the bruising. Otherwise, who knows, I'd have stormed off to the school to find out what was going on and told everyone that he was being bullied, including Will, when Robbie had been telling me the truth all along.

I needed to speak to him when he came home and apologise for not believing him and also try to explain that I worried about him because I cared. I'm sure he'd understand that.

Maybe I did worry too much though. As a single parent I felt a lot more vulnerable than I did when they were two of us.

The responsibility weighed more heavily on my shoulders than it ever did before — and that was something that I would have to explain to Robbie as soon as he came home tonight.

5

Paula Lee, I thought to myself, Paula Deborah Lee. Of course there had to be something at the root of Jack's difficulty to keep up with the business all alone and why he'd neglected his appearance. Why hadn't it entered my thick skull before now that it must be a woman?

A broken heart can do all sorts of crazy things to a person.

I'd found the photograph as I was having a mammoth tidying spree in the office at the sanctuary. It was hidden face down in the bottom of one of the desk drawers, right underneath a pile of copier paper. It must have been slammed down with force at some point, as there was a deep crack across the middle of the glass.

I studied the photo for ages, wondering who she was, gazing at her face which was round and dimpled as a baby's and surrounded by short wispy blonde hair. She smiled straight into the camera in what I thought was a very provocative way.

Her eyes, like two sparkling sapphires edged with thick spiky black lashes, seemed to stare right at me, appraising me and — from her expression — finding me most disappointing. She was very photogenic. I felt that I must ask Jack who she was and whether she had ever been a model.

I recalled Jack's words as we lingered in the office after our first full day of working together — which, incidentally, had been one of the most enjoyable days I'd had for a long time. I showed him the picture and blanching at first, his face as white as a sheet, he told me everything.

'My ex,' he told me. 'We set up the business together — as soon as we saw this place we knew what we wanted to do with it. We got it fairly cheap because it was a bit of a mess, but we worked hard and made it what it is today.

'Paula even named it . . . 'Let's call it Puppy Love,' she said. 'Because this sanctuary is going to be for dogs, no cats or any other animals, only dogs.'

'And that's how it was at the beginning — dogs only, and the name *Puppy Love* was her inspiration from the song that Donny Osmond sang back in the seventies. That song, she said, always meant a lot to her, and Donny did too.

'I think it developed into more than a teenage crush . . . she tried to contact him, sent him letters asking him to marry her for God's sake. And when he eventually married a girl called Debbie, because her middle name is Deborah, she ranted and raved that it should have been her!'

I didn't really know what to say to the comments about her teenage crush. To me it all sounded too much, like the raging of a mad woman. I decided not to mention that, but said that yes, I'd liked the song *Puppy Love* too and that it was a great name for the sanctuary, a name that people certainly wouldn't forget.

He went on to tell me that after about a year together, she'd left him. Just like that, no warning, and he'd never seen or heard from her since.

'Don't get me wrong,' he told me. 'If it had just been the fact that she'd left me, well, OK, I'd have got over it eventually. But she cleared me out — everything, left our bank account totally empty, took every last penny I had — except for a couple of hundred pounds that luckily I'd kept in a separate building society account.' He smiled wryly at me as he said, 'I certainly regretted setting up a joint account with her.

'It was touch and go,' he continued, 'whether or not I would have to close the sanctuary down.'

'So what happened?' I asked him. 'You and the sanctuary are still here, so what happened?'

'Well,' he said, 'It was a bittersweet thing really, Laurel. My dad died very suddenly. He didn't tell me that he'd been suffering from cancer for well over a year, and when he'd gone I found out that he'd left me a substantial amount of money. I'm the only one you see, I've no brothers and sisters, and my mum died years ago ... so there was no one else for him to leave it to.'

'I see,' I said gently, shaking my head sadly. 'Definitely bittersweet ... '

'It saved my life, Laurel,' he said earnestly, looking at me from the depths of his soulful blue eyes. 'And the life of the sanctuary too.'

'How come you say the enterprise is your brainchild?' I asked him. 'After all it was your ex who thought of the name.'

'Oh yes, she thought of the name but that's all. It was my idea to actually set up a sanctuary. Also I funded it with a loan from the bank ... she had no money of her own. When she left me, she not only took all the money from the joint account, but left me with a debt too.'

I shook my head sadly at his words.

Glancing at me, he said, 'But to tell you the truth, the sign did originally have her name on it as well as mine.'

'Were you living together?' I asked him.

'Yes,' Jack said soberly. 'We rented a house in Hampthwaite. I'm still there now. I don't know how long for, though — the rents are pretty high there for a single person so I'm looking for somewhere in either Skelly or Cobby.'

Smiling to myself, I thought, *Hmm, do I need a lodger?* And then I chided myself, thinking, *No — that wouldn't work!*

'Well, I'm sure something will come up,' I told him. 'Will, my ex, got a place in Cobby, a flat above a shop. Maybe I could ask that contact if they have anything else?'

'That would be great, Laurel, thank you,' replied Jack, as we crunched across the car park and I got into my car and Jack into the Puppy Love van to go home.

'See you next Friday?' he asked.

'Yes,' I said. 'See you next Friday.'

I was just about to drive away, that sinking feeling in my tummy that was always there when I had to leave Jack, when suddenly his face appeared at the window of the car.

'Laurel, sorry . . . another favour?'

I smiled and nodded. 'Yes, what is it?

'As you're a hairdresser I wondered if maybe you could give me a hair and beard cut at some time? I feel I really do look like a wild man now! To be paid for, of course!'

'Of course,' I told him. And then feeling really cheeky, I added, 'As long as you pay me in wine and not money.'

'You mean, to buy you a bottle of wine? . . . Or a glass of wine, in a pub?'

'In a pub would be lovely.'

I hoped I wasn't being too pushy but then saw the pleased expression on his face.

'OK then, sounds fair — you're on!' he replied. 'I'll let you know when I can do the makeover,' I said with a grin.

He gave me the thumbs-up as he got into his van and, with a wave, we both drove away.

★ ★ ★

Where on earth is he? I thought as once again I did a tour of the house, looking into every room, the sitting room where usually Alfie could be found lying stretched out like a silky black rug on the floor, or curled as a question mark in the bedroom, or even sitting at his bowl in the kitchen waiting for food. His appetite was insatiable.

'Alfie?' I called, yet there was no answering woof and the urge to see his cute little face became so overwhelming it brought tears to my eyes. 'Alfie?' I called again, a touch hysterically this time, as I ran outside into the garden, almost colliding with Robbie as he came running up the path, followed by a black bounding ball of energy.

'Oh thank God, it's Alfie,' I said. 'Robbie, you really should tell me if you're taking him out with you. I've been looking for him everywhere.'

I bent down and fondled his soft ears revelling in the fact that Alfie was here sitting at my feet, beaming all over his face and his tongue lolling from his mouth. Nothing bad had happened to him. He was safe.

'I didn't take him anywhere,' Robbie said, frowning. 'He came to meet me from school. He was sitting with the mums and dads when I came out into the playground. Dad turned up too,' Robbie told me, his eyes shining with excitement. 'I saw him with one of the teachers, Mum — Mrs Fletcher. It wasn't about me, was it?'

'No, not about you, Robbie,' I said, suddenly feeling a burst of compassion for him. Without thinking — after all he wasn't a baby any more — I held out my arms and Robbie, I'm sure without thinking too, stepped into their safe circle for a hug.

'Sorry, Robbie,' I said, 'It's pretty obvious that you didn't take Alfie out without telling me and that you've just come home from school . . . '

I took in the sight of him in his uniform of black trousers and white shirt, scruffily un-tucked now, overlaid by a bottle-green jumper, the school badge clearly visible on the chest. His jacket drooped untidily from his satchel.

'That's OK, Mum,' he said. Then, pulling himself away from me, he asked, 'I'm starving, what's for tea?'

'Robbie?' I supposed this was as good a time as any to tell him about his dad's girlfriend.

'Yeah?' He looked at me questioningly.

'You said you saw your dad with Mrs Fletcher?' He nodded, a frown on his cute face.

'Well . . . Mrs Fletcher is your dad's girlfriend. He told me about it the other day.'

I held my breath waiting for his reaction. I needn't have worried.

'Oh wow, Mum, she's really pretty. I like Mrs Fletcher. Do you think I might be able to go round her house sometime? With Dad, I mean?' And then before I could reply, 'I'm *really* hungry, can you hear my tummy?'

He pulled my head down so that I could hear the rumbling.

If only everyone was so accepting, I thought as I smiled and ruffled his hair.

'You don't mind, then?'

'No, I think it's really cool.'

'Oh and Robbie — just one more thing.'

'What, Mum?'

'Just to say that I rang your Uncle Rowan because I was worried about those bruises.'

'I told you Mum. I — '

'Yes, yes, hang on, Uncle Rowan explained that you fell against the sideboard, play fighting with Ash. So I'm sorry, Robbie, for doubting you.'

'Oh, that's OK, Mum. Can I have a biscuit or something to last me until tea time? I'm really starving.'

Oh well, I thought. Maybe I don't need to explain everything to Robbie. It seems to me that he knows how much I care without me having to say a word.

Reassured about Robbie but with thoughts of Jack and his ex, Paula; Will and Liz Fletcher; Becky and her new boyfriend, Tom; as well as what we would have for tea racing around in my mind like washing tumbling in a machine, I wearily looked in the pantry to see what we could have.

6

Jack was lying right back in his seat in Cobby Cuts and Curls, his head deeply immersed in the sink and his long legs splayed out in front of him. He had his eyes closed in ecstasy as with my fingertips I gently massaged vanilla-scented soapy bubbles into his scalp.

He looked smart as usual, wearing a pale blue shirt tucked into blue jeans. They had been topped by an old beat-up leather jacket which looked slightly out of place; I'd hung it carefully with the ladies' gowns in the wooden cupboard by the door.

It was my day off really but, after asking Jenny's permission, she said it would be fine, as Wednesday was always quiet, for me to use the facilities in the salon to transform Jack and to give him the make-over of his life!

The radio played softly in the background and I could hear Zoe Ball rambling inanely.

Mrs Wilkinson, Jenny's early morning shampoo and set, stared at Jack as if he were an apparition. He gave her a cheeky grin, showing all his pearly-white teeth, as I showed him to a seat in front of a mirror. He looked like a rather wild bearded Sikh with the white towel piled turban-style on his head.

Outside it was a bright day, the sky blue and the sun a yellow glow, yet a strong, cold wind blew crispy leaves into a frenzy sending them skittering along the pavement and leaving the branches of the trees bare and forlorn.

People walked past battling against the wind and I could hear a dog barking manically in the distance, reminding me of the sanctuary and prompting me to ask the question.

'Who's looking after the sanctuary while you're here?' I asked as I took the towel from Jack's head and, after giving his hair a cursory rub, swapped it for a dry one which I hung carefully around his shoulders and secured with a clip.

'Don't worry, Laurel,' he assured me. 'Kayleigh and Maria, a new volunteer, are holding the fort.' A look of alarm crossed his face on seeing the silver glint of my scissors but he said calmly enough, 'You can't imagine the teasing I got from them this morning when I told them where I was going.'

'I think I can imagine,' I said. 'But they'll get a real shock when they see you this afternoon . . . in fact, they might not even recognise you.' I gazed at him in the mirror giving an impish grin as I waved my scissors, Jack leaning away slightly as if they were an implement of torture! 'Are you ready?'

He nodded and with a nervous smile asked, 'Have I really looked that bad?'

I shook my head and laughed.

'No, I'm exaggerating.'

'Well, go for it . . . '

Thinking of our conversation only the week before when Jack had broached the idea of a beard and hair trim, I asked him teasingly, 'Do you still insist on taking me out for a drink as payment?'

Mrs Wilkinson's head snapped around so suddenly that I was afraid she'd done irreparable damage to her neck.

'Of course. I will take no excuses,' he said easily. 'I'll buy you several large glasses of wine for all your hard work.'

Nodding happily and already tasting the warmth of the red wine on my tongue, I began to snip at his hair, first of all cutting the length which had grown almost to his shoulders and then gradually thinning out the lush curly bulk which fell slowly through the air like confetti, until it was a thick brown mass covering the floor. Then I began shaping it into the nape of his neck.

Gradually, my heart beating nineteen to the dozen, I began to see more of Jack's face — and what a revelation. I know it sounds like a cliché but he really did have chiselled cheekbones just like a hero in a romantic novel. The blue of his eyes seemed to be more pronounced than ever as they stared out from deep sockets which were surrounded by lashes that were not only thick and dark but long too. I would swear that this man wore mascara! I couldn't wait to see the full glory of his jawline and his lips (of which I'd already had a glimpse) which at the moment were still covered by bushy beard.

The salon had become a little busier as Diane had arrived and her first client, a young girl, her hair beautifully straight and glossy, who was booked in for a perm was already sitting in her chair tense with excitement.

'Can you cut it all off and perm it tight and curly?' the girl asked.

Diane, her face a total picture of Why?, hesitated before replying. But then the girl said, 'I want to be different from all the other girls . . .'

I really did sympathise with Diane. Ken Bruce was on the radio now as I could hear the opening bars of the introduction for the Pop Master quiz.

'Clean shaven or designer stubble, Jack?' I asked him.

He contemplated his reflection in the mirror, narrowing his eyes, his head turning from side to side, before saying, 'What do you think is best, Laurel?'

Mrs Wilkinson's sharp ears were fairly twitching, avidly waiting for my reply as Jenny gave the finishing touches to her hairdo and then brandished a mirror so that she could see the back of her head.

'Well, I don't know why, but I do like a bit of stubble.'

'Well, that's what I'll have,' he said decisively, as I set to work slowly and carefully with scissors and razor until the bulk of the beard had disappeared. Jack's square, dimpled jaw was revealed, covered — very artfully now, I thought — with only a sprinkling of stubble.

My heart was beating so hard at the total revelation of Jack that I thought surely he could hear it — or indeed everyone in the salon. But not a word was said and Jack just sat there, staring at himself in the mirror, before finally managing to stammer, 'Well . . . that's a face that I haven't seen properly for a long time. Thank you, Laurel.'

Carefully removing the gown and shaking it out, strands of hair flying through the air and settling on the floor, a sudden image of Jack the very first time I saw him, very attractive but just a bit rough around the edges, flashed through my mind.

'Wow, what a transformation.'

Catching my eye he said, to the intense enjoyment of Mrs Wilkinson and all the other ladies in the salon, 'Well, now that you've done such a good job . . . when can we have that drink?'

* * *

I remember the first time I ever set eyes on Will. I was queuing in the refectory at Cobby College, where I was very happily studying typing and office practice, along with my then two best friends, Imogen and Lisa. It was lunchtime and I was starving, as I always seemed to be. He was just ahead of me and already piling his plate high with some weird-looking concoction cooked up especially for students who really don't know what to eat but always seem to be hungry!

The whole place was manic as usual with students talking and laughing and avidly flirting with one another. But in the midst of all this I couldn't stop staring at him, liking the way he looked and admiring his long, messy hair and skin-tight ripped Levi's, worn with an open-necked shirt, a silver chain tight around the base of his throat, together with a decidedly shabby denim jacket that looked as if it had been through hell and back. Oh, it wasn't old . . . just fashionable.

We shared a table, both of us self-consciously picking at our lunch, and he told me he was studying computer science which was a fairly new course at the time. I was intrigued and secretly thought, because of the word 'computer', that he must be really clever! And of course he was.

Our first date was similar to our rendezvous only the other day — a picnic in Cobby on a bench by the Cenotaph amidst people strolling in the warm summer sunshine or lolling on the benches and shrieking children playing on chunky primary-coloured swings and slides.

We'd been to what was then Cobby's brand new Sparta Supermarket and bought packs of cheese and tomato sandwiches and bars of chocolate that melted to a gooey mess in the heat. We stayed together until late that evening, talking and giggling, secretly drinking sweet cider straight from the bottle, so that without us even noticing, stars in an inky black sky appeared and began to twinkle like tiny silver lights.

He walked me home and we kissed — our first kiss, the cider helping to take the edge off the worry of Mum or Dad suddenly appearing at the front door and 'catching us at it,' as Dad would have said. I remember his lips so soft and gentle and, because of the cider, tasting like apples against my mouth.

The hot night smelled of dry cut grass and petrol fumes from cars cruising by and I became soft as melting wax as he pulled me close, so close I thought he'd never let me go.

What on earth has made that come into my mind? I thought as I gazed at myself in the mirror wondering if I looked OK for my date with Jack. I wore smart jeans and a long-sleeved V-necked black top that felt smooth and silky against my perfumed skin. A pair of high-heeled black shoes completed the outfit as well as a silver choker around my neck and tiny silver hoops in my ears. I carefully scrutinised my hair, where brand new highlights lay amongst the dark like shimmering gold.

My ring finger looked forlornly bare now without my wedding band. Huh — so much for all the lovely times with Will that had now crumbled to nothing but dust. It was strange that neither of us had remembered our first date when we sat by the Cenotaph and had our picnic just the other day. Too much water under the bridge now I suppose, as well as the fact that our minds had been too full of other things —Will telling me that he'd met somebody new and me telling him about Becky's boyfriend.

Putting the past from my mind, I peered from between the curtains to see that it was a dry night but frosty. White patches glinted on the paths and a full moon glowed like a silver coin in a dense black sky. It wasn't far, but I would have to be careful walking into Cobby where I'd arranged to meet Jack in the Star Pub.

The thought of falling on an icy patch and turning up to meet him in a dishevelled mess was certainly not a welcome possibility, not when I had pleasant tingles running up my spine at the thought of a whole evening alone together. The makeover had left him looking far too attractive for his own good, and the possibility of a romance between us was ever-present in my mind.

'Hey, get you,' said Robbie as I walked very carefully, sideways like a crab, in my heels down the stairs. 'Date night! You look really cool, Mum.'

Alfie, I noticed was sitting close to

Robbie, his tongue lolling from his mouth, looking so cute that I stroked his sleek head until he woofed in enjoyment and wagged his tail furiously.

'Thank you, Robbie.' I pulled him towards me and gave him a kiss on the cheek.

He breathed in deeply, wrinkling his nose

'Mmm, you smell nice too.'

Becky's pretty face appeared round the sitting room door. She gave me a scathing look.

'I can't believe you're going for a drink with the Hollywood man.'

I laughed and shook my head. 'It wasn't that long ago that you were quizzing me as to whether or not Jack had a wife! And whether I'd ever go out for a drink with him . . . so your dream has come true!'

She gave a wry smile as I said, 'You should see him now, Becky. He's had a full makeover and looks even more Hollywood. Now, will you two be OK together?'

'Yeah,' she replied. 'I'm gonna watch a film, I think.'

'Is Mandy coming round?' I asked.

She shrugged. 'I might text her to see what she's doing. She'll probably be busy though, I think she's seeing someone at the moment.'

'Oh yeah,' I said teasingly, 'Maybe you can go out as a foursome with her sometime?'

She coloured bright red and said, 'You haven't forgotten that Tom's coming round tomorrow, have you?'

'No, I certainly have not,' I told her. 'I'm looking forward to it.'

'Thanks Mum,' she said. 'Have a good night with the Hollywood man!'

'I certainly hope to,' I answered with a smile.

Robbie with Alfie close at his heels said he was going to his room, so wrapping myself up warmly in a jacket and a scarf, pulling on a pair of fleecy gloves and taking one more nervous check in the mirror, I opened the front door and went out into the night.

'Laurel! Really good to see you. What would you like? Red wine?'

Jack, who had been standing at the bar as I walked into the Star pub, immediately put down his foaming pint and, leaning in close, greeted me with a kiss on the cheek.

'There's a table for two,' he said, pointing. 'How about if we sit there?'

He looked good in black trousers and a smart black jacket, set off by a white open-necked shirt. His shoulders looked broad and I thought of all the muscle on his arms hidden beneath the long sleeves of the jacket. My heart revved up a beat or two.

'Wonderful,' I said as I went and sat down, pulling off my gloves and unbuttoning my jacket. I'd never been in here before so I gazed around, taking in my surroundings. The pub was old and very cosy and welcoming, with dark beams criss-crossing the ceiling and bumpy, dark wooden floors. A fire glowed bright in a shiny wood-burning stove set into a deep fireplace, its mantelpiece being a massive knotty wooden beam blackened to perfection.

Several people milled around the bar area and a few couples sat at tables set with knives and forks and napkins, while several raucous groups stood around drinking, talking and laughing companionably. A strong smell of cooked food hung in the air making me feel quite hungry. If I hadn't already eaten my tea, I would have been tempted to order from what looked like a very extensive menu.

A really old jukebox, the like of which I hadn't seen for years, stood in one corner, rows of vinyl records lined up inside its glass front and a large old-fashioned needle hovering above them. To my surprise there was a sudden whirr and a click. Open-mouthed with fascination, I watched as one of the records dropped down and scratchy music began to play. '*You to me are everything, the sweetest song that I can sing, oh baby . . .*'

The Real Thing, I thought with a sudden

feeling of nostalgia. That song always reminded me of being young and being with Will. I wondered what he was doing and whether he was spending the evening once again with his new girlfriend, Liz.

Thoughts of Will quickly fled my mind as Jack Garthwaite — even more enigmatic since the makeover — walked towards me carrying a pint of beer in one hand and a large glass of red wine in the other. A couple of women at the next table shamelessly ogled him as he put my drink neatly on a beer mat and then, pulling out a chair, sat opposite me and smiled, giving me the full impact of his lovely white teeth and sparkling blue eyes.

'You look very nice, Laurel,' he said appreciatively and then, with a question on his face and his head to one side, asked, 'Dare I say it, but have you had . . . ?' He nodded towards my hair.

I laughed and nodded. 'Yes, I've had some highlights put in — ' I came to an abrupt stop, I didn't want to mention grey hair . . . not to Jack.

I took a deep glug of the wine, which

tasted so rich and fruity I almost kept it in my mouth, rinsing it around and around like a mouthwash.

'It looks very nice,' Jack said with firm approval.

'So does yours,' I said.

'You've made me into a new man.' He leaned closer, putting his forearms on the table, a slice of chest clearly visible. 'Not only with my appearance but the transformation of the sanctuary as well. The office has never been so tidy, and the new website is brilliant!'

'Well, that is my job,' I said modestly. 'But yes, you are a new man — a very attractive new man, I have to say. Just think . . . you've been hidden under that too long hair and beard for how long?'

'Since just after Paula left, I suppose,' he replied. 'Almost a year ago. I didn't have the heart to do anything about it. Not just because she left, but because of the worry over the sanctuary at first, then of course my dad's death . . . all too much for me at once.'

I nodded in sympathy.

'I think you've had a case of mild depression by the sound of it, Jack. After my husband left us I felt the same — I had no interest in the house or . . . well, anything really. I couldn't be bothered to even brush away a cobweb, the spiders had a field day, and, yes, I neglected my appearance for a while too.'

He smiled about the spiders but then said with a frown, 'Your husband left you? I had no idea! I thought you were happily married!'

He took a sip of beer, the froth coating his lips which I could see in all their glory now, causing a pleasant tingle to run through my body. He wiped the froth away with the tip of his finger.

'We've not really discussed anything like that, have we? I've had no reason to mention it but, yes, he left me too, just a little over a year ago.' I glanced at him from beneath my lashes. 'We're still friends though . . . Becky and Robbie live with me but they visit their dad every other weekend and once or twice during the week. He has a flat above Bedrock &

Rose on Cobby High Street.'

Jack shook his head as if in shock

'How long were you married?'

'Almost twenty years,' I told him. 'We met at college, so we were young, probably too young to settle down. The whole thing is for the best though — we were drifting apart, time's rushing by and we're getting older. We're both aware that we need to find happiness elsewhere.'

I blushed at this statement, so much so that I had to raise my glass again and take a deep drink of wine if only to hide my face!

Jack looked at me long and hard, his gorgeous chiselled looks sending shivers running down my spine.

'You won't have any problem there, Laurel, you're a very attractive woman . . . ' And then with a smile, 'And a very nice woman too.'

He raised his drink and I raised mine and we clinked our glasses as if we were celebrating, which I suppose we were, even if it was only Jack's makeover!

I smiled at his words, which would

never have been said if it wasn't for the fact that he'd had a beer. *The truth always comes out when a man drinks*, I remember my mum telling me when I was younger.

'How about your children?' he asked, leaning back in his chair and crossing his legs carefully so as not to crease his trousers, 'How have they taken this separation?'

Another record started playing on the old juke box — Elton John this time, which caused another wave of nostalgia to run through my body. *Goodbye yellow brick road* . . . just as a large group of people walked through the door and started shouting their orders to the two young girls serving at the bar so I could barely hear it!

'Robbie doesn't seem too bad, although I suppose I can be a bit too protective of him at times.' I thought of the bruises on his arm and how I thought he was being bullied at school.

'That's better than not caring, Laurel.'

I nodded. 'Yes I suppose it is . . . but Becky has been very upset. I think she feels that Will, her dad, betrayed her.

She had him right up there on a pedestal,' I said, indicating with my hand way over my head. 'She has a boyfriend now, though, so I'm hoping that will somehow make a difference for her.'

'Aah, first love,' said Jack dreamily. 'What's he like? Have you met him?'

'No, not yet. He's coming round tomorrow for tea so that should be interesting.'

'Hmm, well, I hope he's a nice young man,' he said.

'Yes — I do too,' I murmured, thinking of Tom's brother and the rest of the family who maybe I would get to meet some day, 'I really do too.'

★ ★ ★

The rest of the evening passed in a blur of laughing and talking, with Jack making several more trips to the bar and refusing to take a single penny from me, insisting that he'd had the makeover of his life and wanted to make sure that I was well paid for it!

Curious about a comment that Jack had made earlier, I asked him, 'If you thought I was happily married, why did you ask me to go out for a drink with you?'

He shifted his gaze away slightly before saying heartily, 'To repay you for the makeover, of course!'

I nodded as if I totally understood and took another sip of wine, just as a bell jangled and the girl serving behind the bar shouted, 'Last Orders at the bar please, last orders at the bar.'

A milling throng of people, a look of sheer panic on their faces, raced to surround her.

Jack walked me home, his arm tight around my waist, both of us slipping and sliding drunkenly on the white frosty paths. The sky arched above us like a deep black cavern studded with tiny twinkling stars and the air so fresh and cold numbed my intoxicated brain.

Jack's taxi to his rented house in Hampthwaite arrived almost straight away and I felt the brush of his sexy stubble against my cheek and then my lips as he kissed me good night.

I stood shivering at the garden gate, my heart beating fast, watching the tiny red lights of the car as they receded into the distance.

7

The sun awoke me the next morning, shining through the curtains and pooling on the floor and the duvet in long golden stripes.

The kisses which in my dreams were from the enigmatic Jack Garthwaite — warm, tender kisses that caressed my face and my neck slowly and erotically making me moan in delight, turned out to be from the lolling tongue of Alfie the black Labrador. Turning away slightly from his imploring stare and closing my eyes again, I really didn't want to get up just yet. I once again conjured up a vision of Jack, his juicy lips moving closer and closer to mine and the sexy rasp of his stubble against my cheek. Would I ever be lucky enough for kisses like that to happen again?

I thought of Jack's ex, Paula, and wondered why she had left him so suddenly. What had he done? Or not done? What had been the reason? Thinking of our night out together and the intelligence of our conversation, his wit and his sexiness, I couldn't imagine why any woman would ever want to leave him!

Obviously I was biased. I only knew his version of events and not hers. Maybe I would change my mind about him if I knew the whole story? If there was a whole story . . . but who knows!

My phone, vibrating madly on the bedside cabinet, brought me out of my reverie as did the excited woofing of Alfie, as, almost jumping out of his fur at the mobile's antics and eyeing it warily, he very slowly sat back on his haunches, his tail wagging furiously.

'Hi Laurel, it's Maggie . . . sorry for ringing so early. It's just that Stephen and I are out in the garden and I suppose it's because of all the rain we've been having — but the grassed area is a bog! Do you remember anything being said about these houses being built on a flood plain?'

'Nobody said anything to me before

I moved in,' I told her. 'But I did hear later, and they certainly should have done if there's a problem.'

'I'm going to have it brought up by council,' she told me. 'I knew that it was a much maligned new estate because of the green belt issue, but not that it was on a flood plain!'

'Oh yes — you're a councillor, aren't you, Maggie?' I said, fully awake now.

'Yes, I am. Maybe I could speak with Kath's husband Paul Timpson. He's a planning officer and might know something about it.'

'Yes, that's a good idea. How did it go ahead when there were complaints about the green belt though?'

'I've no idea, Laurel. The planning officers don't seem to listen. For example, they knew that the residents of Cobby didn't want a Sparta Supermarket, but we got one anyway, didn't we?'

'Yeah, you're right there!'

'My mum campaigned against that. She was worried about the impact the big supermarket would have on our small local Yarrows. And, of course, she was right and Sparta took most of their business away.'

'It's not fair, Maggie, it really isn't. I'll have a look in my garden when I get downstairs and see if mine's boggy as well.'

'OK, yes, let me know. I'll call in to the office to see Kath later as well — she might advise me what to do. Those builders, they just build anywhere nowadays, don't they?'

'Yes, they have to build a certain amount of houses per year apparently. So, flood plain or not, they're going to build — and green belt? What's that?'

I hung up on Maggie's call with a sinking heart and without further ado, jumped out of bed and went to investigate my garden, Alfie trotting along at my side. I hummed to myself as I ran down the stairs, '*Me and my shadow, strolling down the avenue . . .*'

★ ★ ★

The ground was rocky beneath my trainers as I ran; the sleek black shape of Alfie a blur at my side. He was panting, his tongue hanging so far from his mouth that I was afraid he might trip over it.

It was a dank afternoon, verging on darkness, the smoky smell of autumn in the air, as we'd set off from home at a steady trot into Cobby Village, past Bloomers the Bakers and its straggling queue, past Cobby Cuts and Curls, the aroma of shampoo and conditioner sneaking like a mist out of the door, and then past Bedrock & Rose where I took a quick glance up at Will's flat and the balcony where his plants cascade down as thick and heavy as a tumbling green waterfall.

Thoughts ran through my mind. The up and coming visit on Saturday from Tom, Becky's boyfriend; Robbie wondering if seeing his dad with one of the teachers meant that he'd done something wrong; and now all this business with a boggy garden, for yes, mine was just as bad! According to Maggie, Kath was going to ask Paul Timpson if he could call round to Maggie's place to look at the garden and obviously mine now too.

Apparently it was Paul Timpson who was given the job when the application for a new housing development came into the office but one of his colleagues took over and, as yet, we weren't sure why. Time would tell, I supposed.

Alfie and I were running along the towpath now, the canal brown and sluggish at our side and the sky one giant bronze cloud mirroring the water and hiding the sun. Ducks and regal white swans, their beaks a shiny orange V in the gloom, swam past, their skinny legs moving rapidly in the water, in and out, in and out like an accordion. Bad-tempered geese hissed and spat but Alfie ignored them, head down, too intent on his run to retaliate.

Leaving the canal behind we turned up a steep, narrow lane overgrown with long grass and nettles that brushed softly against my bare legs, leaving stinging red marks which at the moment I could barely feel. I was almost on tiptoes now, the muscles in my legs screaming in agony the higher I climbed, my stomach muscles clenching and my breath rasping in my throat until like Alfie I was panting. Thankfully the ground began to flatten out and I could see in the distance the trig point — Cobby Cairn, as the locals call it. A squat stone structure that stands at the highest point for miles around, which has the most breathtaking views imaginable.

The thought of getting to the trig point occupied my mind, pushing away any worrying thoughts as I pressed on, my heart pumping like a piston, the dark shape of Alfie hovering at the edge of my vision. Endorphins exploded into my brain like fireworks at New Year as I ran the last few steps and reached out to touch the stones, which felt cool and reassuring beneath my fingertips.

Leaning over, my hands on my thighs, breathing heavily, I took a couple of minutes' break before setting off downwards, running as carefully as I could in the gloom, Alfie just ahead of me, his floppy ears flattened to his head in the strong breeze.

Uneasy thoughts of Jack began to run through my mind and I found myself wondering why I hadn't heard from him since our night out the week before. I'd half expected an early morning text and had spent most of the following day stealing glances at my phone, waiting for the little message icon to appear on the screen. But it had stayed dark, blank, and unresponsive.

Well, I thought, *he did say from the beginning that he was only buying me a drink as payment for the makeover . . .*

I felt stupid now that I'd hoped for more. What a silly romantic I was. Heaving a heartfelt sigh I carried on running, my legs tired now and heavy as lead. Hopefully the situation would become clearer the following day when I saw him at the sanctuary.

* * *

It was dark when Alfie and I arrived home, the air dense and suffocating as I opened the door and stepped into the hallway. Becky's face appeared, peering over the banister like a pale hanging globe. Squinting, I looked up at her, Alfie still panting at my side.

Her voice sounded light and musical. 'Mum . . . Tom texted me tonight.'

My heart, still racing from the run, sped up again and the rapidly cooling sweat that coated my skin made me shiver.

'Why? What's happened? Nothing bad I hope?'

'Nothing,' she replied with a giggle in her voice. 'He's just really looking forward to visiting us on Saturday.'

'Naughty, I thought something had happened!'

'Just teasing . . . '

I gave her a wry smile and, climbing the stairs towards her, headed to the bathroom for a shower.

★ ★ ★

A car I'd never seen before was parked in the stony car park at the sanctuary when I arrived the next morning. It was a Mini, bright red and shiny, with luxury black leather seats. I noticed it had a private number plate ending in DEB.

Deb . . . Debbie? Deborah? My heartbeat quickened and I frowned as, with a strange suspicion eating away at me, I picked up my bag from the passenger seat and got out of the car. I noticed that Jack's van was there and in its usual place.

The weather hadn't improved since yesterday. It was still dank and dark, the sky a great mass of dull cloud. Even as I hurried over to the office building, pulling my hood over my hair, a fine misty rain began to fall.

Going straight into the office, I saw Jack immediately, sitting in his usual place at his desk. He was bending over some papers spread out over the computer keyboard where a woman with very short blonde hair was leaning over him, pointing at something with her finger.

The nail, I noticed, was long and square-ended and painted a bright scarlet.

She turned as she heard the door opening and gave a bright, white smile that didn't quite meet her eyes.

'Ah, Laurel,' said Jack, jumping up straight away. 'Is it Friday already? Time does fly. Umm . . . this is Paula. Paula, this is Laurel.'

Oh, so this is Paula — the photogenic woman from the damaged picture. She looked very different from that photograph. Her face had filled out considerably, so she'd lost that impish sort of gamine quality she'd had previously that went so well with her short blonde hair. Although, looking at the style with my hairdresser's eye, the cut could be a lot better.

She was the woman who had done Jack so much wrong, and now he'd more or less said that he'd forgotten I was coming in today. Was that said for Paula's benefit or was he so wrapped up with her, that he really had forgotten about me? Was he showing his true colours? Was the lovely Jack Garthwaite a figment of my imagination?

Feeling sick and down at heart, I pasted a smile on my face and held out my hand.

'Hi Paula, I'm Laurel, pleased to meet you.'

'Pleased to meet you,' she said shortly, touching the tips of my fingers fleetingly with her own as if I was something nasty. 'Laurel? That's weird! Sounds more like a garden plant than a name.' She gave a silvery tinkle of a laugh.

Jack frowned at her and said chidingly, 'Come on Paula, be nice!'

'Yes,' I said reasonably. 'It is a garden plant, a hedging plant actually. I'm very lucky to have an unusual mother who gave both her children distinctive names. My brother is called Rowan! A rowan is a tree, by the way.'

Yeah, put that in your pipe and smoke it, I thought to myself.

'Ooh, get you . . . that's wonderful! I'm just plain old Paula.'

'That's not plain at all,' I said nicely.

'Now I really should be getting on with some work. Jack, what would you like me to do this morning?'

'If you could carry on with updating the dog records, Laurel; that would be a great help.'

★   ★   ★

The morning passed quickly. I was soon immersed with updating the records as Jack had asked me to, in addition to answering telephone queries and dealing with people as they came to view the animals. It was so rewarding when somebody did actually adopt a dog or a cat and I was lucky enough to see the animal off in their little carrying baskets, sometimes timid and shy, sometimes cocksure and fancy-free, but always so grateful, I felt sure, to be on the way to their new forever home.

The only fly in the ointment was Paula hanging around Jack's desk, leaning over him and whispering God knows what in his ear as he worked. Or tried to work!

Most of her top half seemed to be in his face from what I could see.

I was hoping upon hope that Jack would have a word with me later and tell me what was going on and why she was here. Had they resumed their relationship? Had she come back to check on the business or, indeed, be part of it again? I felt that as I worked here now, I should be informed of all these things.

Lunchtime neared and Jack said, 'You go off and get some lunch if you like, Laurel. You deserve a break, updating records can be tedious work.'

I gave him a thin smile. 'OK — I will, thank you.'

I went into the little kitchen that we used at break and lunchtimes and immediately put the kettle on. Going to my bag, I pulled out the sandwiches that I'd brought with me. After making a drink, I sat down at the little Formica-topped table and opened up a book — *Rebecca* by Daphne Du Maurier — and settled down to eat and read together. One of my favourite pastimes!

Just as I was getting to an exciting part of the book, where Mrs 'awful' Danvers had the poor second wife in Rebecca's bedroom scaring her half to death, Paula sashayed in, her wide hips undulating beneath her too-short dress. She wasn't the slimmest person in the world and wore the dress pulled tight at the waist with a chunky belt making it appear even shorter. Also it was very low-cut giving what you might call a broad view of her top half!

Going straight to the kettle, she said, 'Ooh, a reader, are you?' And before I could reply, she went on, 'I hate reading. I find it a total waste of time. Time when I could be doing so many other things!'

'Oh,' I replied coolly, 'I find it stimulates the brain and gives so much to think about — especially if it's good literature, as this book is.'

Peering over my shoulder she read, '*Rebecca* by Daphne Du what?' She gave her usual tinkling laugh.

'Daphne Du Maurier,' I said. 'She wrote lots of books — she was really very talented.'

The kettle bubbled to the boil and I was aware of her pouring water into her cup. I heard the tinkling of a spoon against the mug. The thought *I hope she goes now* ran through my mind, but, no, she sat down at the table opposite me.

As she placed her mug down with a thud, she asked menacingly, 'Why are you here, Laurel?'

Surprised, I looked up and met her piercing blue eyes.

'What do you mean?'

'Are you after Jack?'

'After Jack?' I asked, astounded.

'Yes, Jack told me you'd split up from your husband and that you're a single parent with two children. Are you after a meal ticket or something?'

She took a casual sip from her mug leaving a lipstick mark, red and oily, on its surface.

Rage rose red hot inside me but I tried to calm myself and replied icily, 'I have been apart from my husband for the best part of a year now, Paula, and can manage quite well on my own. Jack advertised for an admin assistant and I got the job. End of!'

'OK, keep your hair on,' she said. 'I'm only asking. I need to know the score and Jack is pretty tight-mouthed.'

'There's nothing for Jack to tell you,' I replied. 'I work for him one day a week and that's it!'

'That's good. No doubt Jack has told you about me? I set up this business with him and I put in a lot of hard work — so why should he get all the benefit?'

'That's none of my business,' I informed her.

'No, you're right, it isn't!'

There was a short silence in which I stood up, threw away the foil from my sandwich, put the container back in my bag and closed my book with a thud.

'What Jack doesn't know yet,' she told me, a smirk on her face, idly stirring her coffee with the tinkling spoon, 'Is that one of the reasons I disappeared was to have his baby. He has a daughter — she's three months old. I named her Jacqueline for him . . .'

I stared at her wide-eyed and open-mouthed for, if that was true, I'd lost Jack before anything had even started.

'Oh dear, you do look shocked, Laurel! What is it? Don't people in your perfect little world get pregnant out of wedlock?'

Ignoring her nasty comments, I said coldly, 'Don't you think you should be speaking to Jack about such a thing?'

'Oh, don't worry, I will be,' she said, with a pointed smile, 'And then no doubt I'll move back in with him and he won't need an admin assistant at all. Jack and I will work together again.'

She sat back in her seat, shoulders thrust forward and showing far too much of her chest area.

'Don't worry, Paula, it's no skin off my nose,' I said carelessly. 'I'm quite happy as I am with my two children and my dog, and my job as a hairdresser that I thoroughly enjoy.'

She gave me a scathing glance as I stood up, neatly pushing my chair under the table.

'Oh, and by the way,' I said, staring at her sulky face. 'If you ever feel the need for a good haircut, I'll do it for you! And, as we have a mutual friend, I'll even give you a discount!'

'Oh, go away,' she said petulantly, as, quite pleased with myself, I swept from the room.

8

It was Saturday and we were waiting for Becky's boyfriend, Tom, to come round. I'd prepared my culinary masterpiece, spaghetti bolognaise, with accompanying garlic bread and set the dining room table with the best cutlery and napkins. Oh yes, I'd gone the whole hog.

I'd also made a blackberry and apple crumble which Alfie (and even Robbie) had been looking at longingly for the past hour, Alfie sniffing the air with his long, black nose.

Becky had dressed herself up to the nines wearing new skinny jeans that fit her like a glove and one of her cold shoulder tops in a beautiful emerald green, which really brings out the colour of her eyes. She'd artfully made up her face with black eyebrows and lashes, and a rich, creamy pink lipstick.

Girls seem to be so much better at make-up these days. When I was sixteen I didn't even wear any! I remember watching my mum, and getting ideas from her, as she made up her face with blue or green eyeshadow and long, sweeping lines around her eyes like Cleopatra!

Even Robbie had smartened himself up by wearing a pair of clean jeans and a shirt instead of his usual crumpled T-shirt that I always call his fashionable just-got-out-of-bed look.

Alfie also looked pretty cool, wearing his own personalised dog bandana in bright red, which looked good against his black fur, embroidered with his name in white swirly letters.

I'd taken the opportunity to make myself look presentable. With the return of Paula to the sanctuary, I didn't think there would be many more opportunities for me to get dressed up to go out with Jack. And with the bombshell that she'd dropped about Jack's baby (I know it's mean-spirited but I have to say it — if it really *is* Jack's baby), and the certainty that she would be moving back in with him, I had no idea what the future held for me at all! It was a pity because I'd had a word with Maggie about accommodation in the Cobby area and her sister, Lynette, was looking out for places with Jack in mind. He maybe wouldn't need anywhere now.

The day had been dreary and overcast and when six o'clock came it was pitch black outside. There was a roar of an engine and, peering from the sitting room window, I could just about see Becky fly down the garden path. Unfortunately the tall hedge that encircled the garden made it impossible to see anything so, the possible lover's clinch that was going on right now, was not witnessed by me. However Robbie must have been able to see them from the bedroom window as, his voice echoing down the stairs, provided a running commentary.

'Oh no, they're kissing, Mum . . . oh and, Mum, guess what, he's got a motorbike! It's bright red and looks really ace!'

My heart sank, although I'd suspected as much when I'd heard the roar of an engine. After all, what else could it be? I was surprised, though, as Tom was only seventeen. Was it legal for him to ride a motorbike?

'Mum, we're here.' Becky's voice sailed in through the front door and into the hallway. There was a kerfuffle and a bit of giggling as she helped Tom take off his coat and hang it up and then they appeared in the sitting room doorway.

'How do you do, Tom,' I said as a good-looking young man walked towards me. He had short, dark hair and a swarthy skin and was stocky with wide, powerful-looking shoulders. He had a good, firm grip as he shook my hand which I liked. 'A good firm handshake gives a favourable impression of a person,' my dad always said. Unlike Paula's, that tiny feather-light swipe of her fingers on mine, as if she could barely bring herself to touch me! Hmm, now what did that mean?

'Mrs Masters, it's really good to meet you. Wow . . . Becky looks just like you!'

'Oh, please, call me Laurel. 'Mrs Masters' makes me feel old! Good to meet you, Tom. Do we really look so alike? Please sit down . . . '

I indicated the sofa.

'This is Alfie,' said Becky, putting a protective arm around him as he came to sit beside them, his tongue lolling out and a smile on his face. 'Yeah,' she said, frowning. 'Do I really look so much like my mum?'

'You do,' said Tom, 'Like twins! Hi there, Alfie . . . ' He gently rubbed his sleek neck. 'Becky says that Alfie runs with you?'

'Albeit I'm the much older twin,' I said with a grin. 'Yes, Alfie is the best running partner I've ever had.'

'Hi, I'm Robbie,' said a little voice and Robbie wandered into the sitting room and sat down, giving a shy nod towards Tom.

'Hey there, man,' said Tom, going over and giving Robbie's hand a hearty shake. 'How ya doing?'

'Oh — fine, thanks,' replied Robbie, colouring slightly.

'Yeah, he's my baby bro,' said Becky proudly.

'Hey! I'm no baby,' exclaimed Robbie, shyness forgotten.

'I've heard so much about all of you, that I feel as if I know you already,' Tom stated.

'Yes, and I about you, Tom,' I said carefully. 'But there's just one thing that Becky didn't tell me . . . '

Becky looked wary, almost shifty-eyed, and moved along the settee closer to Tom.

Robbie suddenly piped up, 'If it's about the motorbike, Mum, it's really ace, a brilliant bright red — oh, and the registration number is really cool!'

All three of us looked at Robbie in wonder. 'What about the registration number?' I asked him.

'Your Hollywood man would love it for his dog sanctuary, it's DO16 PUP. How about that, then?' He gave one of his childish giggles and we all laughed and Becky said, 'Wow, that's really cool!'

'I can tell by your face that it won't cut it though, will it, Mum? I'll go put the kettle on. Would you all like tea or coffee?'

I raised my eyebrows at Robbie for his kind suggestion and he blushed poppy red again. Everybody nodded yes please and once Robbie was gone, Tom turned to me and said, 'I think I know the problem. I take it you didn't know I had a motorbike?'

'No, I didn't,' I told him. 'I would absolutely hate for Becky to go on a motorbike.'

'No worries,' he told me, 'I can't take a pillion passenger until I'm nineteen anyway, but as I'm seventeen I can ride a 125cc bike. I've passed my theory test now so don't need L-plates, which is great. I love my bike, Mrs . . . um, I mean Laurel, and I'm real careful, and, as well as that, I would never harm Becky.'

He fumbled for her hand and gripped it tightly.

They smiled at each other.

'I don't want to ride pillion anyway, Mum,' she told me sincerely. 'I'd be too scared.'

'Well,' I shrugged. 'Who can tell, if you're still together in two years' time, you might want to . . . but let's cross that bridge when we come to it.'

'Two years?' said Becky in disbelief. 'Two years is forever, Mum!'

'Oh, it will soon go,' I told them, with all the weight of my forty-seven years on my shoulders.

As far as I was concerned the evening was a success and all my worries about Becky having a boyfriend melted away.

I told Becky that she should take Tom to meet her dad, stressing to her how happy that would make him. She shrugged, an impatient gesture; that told me that perhaps she wasn't ready to do that as yet.

Oh well, time would tell! I would fill Will in on the evening as I said I would and hopefully, who knew, he might be able to wheedle some information from her.

* * *

Maggie had just rung to let me know that Paul Timpson, Kath's husband and local planning officer, was round at her place inspecting her boggy garden and maybe he could look at mine while he was nearby? Peeking from the window I see a man in Maggie's garden wearing a beanie hat, black leather gloves and a long dark overcoat. He was pressing a booted foot to the bog and shaking his head while talking avidly to Maggie.

I noticed that he had very dark brown eyes and attractive stubble around his jaw and his cheeks, just like Jack's. It looked to me as though Kath was a very lucky woman which, once again, made me wonder if Maggie had got it right when she told me that Kath had talked to her dead husband for many months after he died. I suppose it was her way of coping.

Gazing again at Paul Timpson and indulging my envy of Kath for meeting such a lovely man to help her over her husband's death, made me feel sorry for myself at being booted out so soon by the gorgeous Jack Garthwaite in favour of his nasty ex, Paula. There's no accounting for taste, is there?

Hurrying outside I introduced myself over the garden fence and waited until both Paul Timpson and Maggie came into my garden. Paul gave me a charming smile and shook my hand, a good firm handshake — I expected no less from him — and proceeded to test the boggy area of my garden with his booted foot, once again shaking his head as if quite annoyed with the whole situation.

It was a miserable, cold day with spits and spots of rain in the air. Hugging my arms around myself I envied Paul Timpson his nice warm-looking overcoat but joined him at the boggy patch and tested it with my foot just as he was doing. My trainer was swallowed up immediately by freezing cold water and I gasped.

He gave me a wry smile and nodded.

'Yes, you have got a problem, haven't you?' I nodded cringing at my cold foot.

'When the application for this new build came into the office,' he told us, 'It was given to me. I advised that because of green belt and with the area being a flood plain that it shouldn't go ahead. Unfortunately, the application was taken away from me and passed on to a colleague. And that was it, I'm afraid, I had no more to do with it. To tell you the honest truth, I only came here today because Kath asked me to.' He gave a little grimace. 'Otherwise I might have been tempted to keep well out of it.'

'Well,' I said. 'That was very sneaky of them, Mr Timpson. They obviously wanted it to go through, so more or less sacked you from the job!'

'Yes.' He nodded. 'Please, um . . . ?'

'Laurel,' I told him.

'Please, Laurel, call me Paul . . . you've summed it up correctly.'

'I want to take it to council,' declared Maggie. 'Will you speak at the meeting, Paul?'

'What do you want me to say, Maggie?'

'What you've just told us — that the area is green belt and a flood plain, and that houses shouldn't have been built here!'

'Can I think about this?' he asked us, looking at us both with those very deep brown eyes.

'Of course,' replied Maggie.

'It's just that I don't know what sort of a hornet's nest I might be raking up. Do you understand?'

We both nodded but then I said, 'But we could tell the council what you've just told us, couldn't we?'

'Yes, you could but I'd prefer it if my name wasn't mentioned.' After a pause he said, 'This would be a different scenario if I wasn't still working for the council — if, for example, I was self-employed, or retired even!' And once again with a raising of the eyebrows, he said, 'I hope you understand?'

We both nodded and then Maggie said, 'Well, something needs to be done. Will you let us know whether or not you will speak, Paul?'

'Yes I will,' he replied, delving into the pocket of his coat and handing us a business card before we escorted him around to the front of the house. We watched him as he walked down the garden path, fumbling in his pocket for a packet from which he took a cigarette before getting into his car and giving us a cheery wave as he drove away.

'Hmm,' said Maggie, turning to me and giving me a wide-eyed smile, 'Such an attractive man . . . '

'Yes,' I replied, 'Just what I was thinking . . . I hope he will come to council on our behalf. Do you think he will?'

'I'm not sure,' she said, 'I'll let you know if I hear from him, and indeed when the whole thing can go to council. Something will have to be done though, Laurel.'

'Yes, I suppose it will, although fitting a pump would do to get rid of that water.'

'No,' replied Maggie, forcefully. 'That shouldn't be our job. The council or the builders should sort it out for us!'

'Yes — but what if they won't? What if too much time has gone by? What if it's too late?'

'Well, I very much hope not!' She glared at me, 'I'm going to fight this, Laurel, really fight it, right to the bitter end!'

Cobby Cuts and Curls was busy and I was having a quick break in between stages of putting a colour on my client's hair. My phone suddenly pinged and, looking closer, I see it's a message from Jack.

Hmm, I thought. *How unexpected . . . now what does he want?*

Hi Laurel, his message ran, *hope you are well? Would it be possible to see you? I know you're at work today but could you meet when you've finished, maybe in The Star? I really need to talk to you. J x*

Needing to get back to my client, I replied straight away, *OK, how about 6pm in The Star as you suggested?*

I waited for a few minutes hoping that he'd get back quickly. Sure enough, my phone pinged.

That's great. 6pm is good. See you there. J x

I spent the rest of the day in a state of nervousness, wondering what on earth he wanted to talk to me about. It surely had to be about Paula. The ex who has suddenly turned up out of the blue. The ex who treated him so badly he didn't have the heart to get his own hair trimmed for almost a year. What on earth was I going to say to him?

★   ★   ★

The time went by in a blur and before I knew what I was doing, I was walking into The Star pub, my heart beating ferociously and my stomach in knots.

Jack came over to me straight away from where he stood at the bar, a pint of foaming beer in one hand and a glass of red wine in the other.

'Laurel,' he said. 'Thank you for coming . . . there's a table over there . . . shall we?'

I nodded and followed him over to the table where we sat down. I hung my coat over the back of the chair, took off my hat and gloves and put them on the table. He set down a beer mat and carefully placed the red wine on it in front of me.

'Cheers,' he said, raising his pint glass.

'Cheers,' I said. 'Thank you for the wine. Now, how can I help?'

'Oh Laurel, please don't be formal with me. It's Paula that I need to talk to you about . . . I didn't know she was coming back. She turned up at the house on Sunday morning, the day after our night out. I couldn't believe it. She was the last person I thought I'd ever see again.

'I tried to talk to you when you came in to work on Friday but Paula was always around. That's why I asked to meet you tonight.'

'Really,' I said coldly, taking a sip of wine. 'You perhaps didn't try hard enough! For one thing, you should have told me that she was back working at the sanctuary. I had no idea what was going on, Jack! And anyway, it appeared to me that you weren't even bothered about me being there on Friday. You made a comment when I arrived to the effect, 'Oh, is it Friday already . . .''

He gazed at me with his beautiful blue eyes, 'That was just a throwaway comment that meant nothing, Laurel. Just that . . . I don't know . . . time flies! But to correct your impressions — Paula is not back working at the sanctuary. I wanted to tell her to sling her hook, but I thought, *no, I'll wait and see what she wants first. I'll wait and see what trouble she's going to cause this time.*

'But she was sort of OK, by her standards — unbelievably rude to you, of course, I had a word with her about that — '

I stayed silent. I was waiting for him to mention the baby, his daughter — Jacqueline, whom Paula had told me about.

He gazed at me again, his look assessing, obviously wondering what I was thinking. He leaned forward, his elbows on the table between us. Oh if only he wasn't so attractive.

'The thing is though, Laurel, she told me that she has a baby, three months old, and well . . . '

'That she's yours?' I asked.

'How did you know that? That's what she told me, yes!'

The door suddenly opened and a group of people came in, laughing and talking in loud voices, the jukebox started up with a song that I hadn't heard for years.

If you leave me now, you'll take away the biggest part of me . . . The words touched my heart just as they always had. *Ooh no, baby, please don't go . . .*

'Do you believe her?' I said loudly over the din.

He took a sip of beer.

'I'm not sure . . . what do you think, Laurel?'

'Me? Why do you ask me? I've no idea!'

Angrily I took a deep glug of wine this time.

'You've met her — what do you think?'

'Do you really want to know?' I asked, sitting up straight in my seat now, anger simmering just below the surface, red hot and rapidly coming to the boil.

'Yes, I do,' he said, even though a look of alarm flared in his blue eyes.

'I think she's rude and obnoxious,' I told him. 'I think she's taking you for a ride and lying to you by telling you that the baby is yours. Now if you'll please excuse me, Jack, but I have things to do . . .'

I stood up and began to put on my coat. I picked up my gloves and hat from the table.

He stood up and put out his hands.

'Laurel, please, no, don't go, please . . .' He looked worried, distraught even.

'Also, Jack, it's probably better that I don't come to the sanctuary any more — I can't stand this situation. But don't worry, I'll send my written notice. Now I really must go!'

Leaving the remains of the glass of wine he'd bought me — I definitely didn't want it now — I grabbed my bag.

Leaning towards me, Jack gripped my arm. 'No, Jack,' I said, the tone of my voice letting him know in no uncertain terms that he should let me go.

Reluctantly he loosened his grip. Nastily I pulled my arm away and left the pub without a backward glance.

9

Arriving home, I collapsed in a shaking heap on the settee, tears flowing now and running down my face and no doubt mascara too so that I looked like a female version of that seventies rocker, Alice Cooper.

What had I done?

It had started to rain and I could hear the relentless drumming of raindrops on the windows and on the roof. I thought briefly of the boggy garden and whether or not this fresh spate of rain would make the situation worse than ever.

Alfie followed me as I padded into the kitchen, shrugging out of my coat on the way. I made myself a cup of coffee, strong and black. It ran through my veins giving me strength and restoring me to some sort of rational thought.

How glad I was that Becky was doing homework with Mandy and that Robbie was with Ash playing computer games — and thank God that Becky had walked Alfie earlier so I wouldn't have to take him out now. Although I supposed really that a walk would have done me good . . . even in the pouring rain.

I patted Alfie's silky head as, absent-mindedly, I took a sip of coffee. He retired back to his bed, kept warm and cosy by its situation next to the radiator. He lay down, curling up into a ball and closing his eyes, obviously worn out by the long walk he'd had earlier.

I was glad I was alone — I wouldn't have wanted Becky or Robbie to see me like this, crying and acting like a woman gone mad!

With a sudden spurt of energy and before I could change my mind, I got out my laptop and quickly typed out my notice of resignation to Jack. It took me all of five minutes. I pressed send straight away, watching it go from the inbox to the sent box in the blink of an eye.

Well, it's too late now, I thought. *No more working at the sanctuary.*

I'd got so attached to the animals that

the thought of never seeing them again brought tears to my eyes and I began to weep all over again. What a stupid woman I was. In a way I knew that I was better off out of it — but only because of the return of a certain person.

At least I wouldn't have to look at Paula's simpering face ever again. Or be insulted as if I was an inferior — or something that had stuck to the bottom of her shoe!

I thought about the few personal belongings that were still there at the sanctuary and thought that perhaps I could drop in early one morning before Jack arrived. I could let myself in, collect my things and then post the key back through the door . . .

The beeping of my phone alerted me to a text.

It was from Jack.

I do not accept your resignation, Laurel. Please report to work on Friday at 9am as per your contract. J

'No way,' I shouted into the silent house as angrily I threw my phone as far as it would go across the room.

Sobbing into my hands, I didn't hear the front door open nor the tread of footsteps along the hallway until a voice said, 'Mum, what's wrong?'

'Oh Robbie,' I said, looking at him standing in the doorway like a lost soul. He wore a waterproof coat with the hood pulled up over his head. His face was wet with raindrops.

He threw his arms around me, squashing me against him, his soggy coat soaking my skirt and my top.

'If that Hollywood man has upset you, Mum, I'll get him for you.' He broke away from me and went across the room to retrieve my phone. Clenching it in his fist and shaking it, he said sternly, 'Mum, you could have broken this . . . you'd have really missed your phone, wouldn't you?'

I nodded, unable to speak, when all of a sudden my phone began to ring, pulsing in my hand, and making me jump. My heart beat harder at the thought that it might be Jack, having another go at me about my resignation, but the screen lit up showing the name *Becky*. I scrabbled to answer the call.

'Hello? Becky?'

'Oh Mum, please come, I was on my way home . . . there's been an accident just down the road and the police are here . . . it's mayhem, oh my God, Mum, it's Tom's bike all smashed up . . . there's an ambulance too . . . '

'Keep calm, Becky,' I told her, 'I'm on my way . . . are you sure it's Tom's bike?'

'Yes, it's the registration, it stuck with me what Robbie said, DO16 PUP . . . please hurry up, Mum.'

The first thought I had was that I was so happy that Becky hadn't been riding pillion and then another thought came to me, as I prepared to leave the house, Robbie close behind me, *How glad I was that I didn't drink all the wine Jack had bought me in the pub!*

Well . . . they do say that things happen for a reason.

Cringing as the first drops hit us like bullets, Robbie and I ran out into the rain.

* * *

The ambulance was just moving away from the scene, lights flashing and siren blaring, as I arrived. I saw Becky straight away, standing on the pavement, shoulders hunched to her ears, shivering violently while talking to two police officers.

Rushing over to her, Robbie behind me, I heard one of the officers saying, 'They've taken him to the hospital, Miss.'

'But I'm his girlfriend,' I heard her cry plaintively. 'Why couldn't I have gone with him?'

The other police officer pointed out reasonably, 'But Miss, there was no ID on him. He hasn't been identified yet.'

'It's his bike,' she said almost hysterically.

Looking up, Becky saw me and Robbie and ran over to us, hurling herself into my arms.

'Oh Mum, please hurry, we'll have to go to the hospital.'

She was soaked through, her hair

hanging in her eyes a stringy mess and her mascara, so carefully applied this morning, black rings around her eyes.

'They wouldn't let me go in the ambulance with him,' she told me over and over again.

I turned her around and guided her to start walking.

'Quickly, get in the car. The sooner we get to the hospital the better.'

As we passed the scene, a quick glimpse showed just a heap of metal glinting in the street lights. The police car's blue lights flashed eerily. Becky white-faced beside me, started to sob.

'He must be really hurt, don't you think?'

Before I could reply, Robbie, who was leaning forward from the back seat, gently patted his sister on the shoulder and said, 'Nah, don't worry, Becky, he's probably just got a broken leg or something like that. Something easily mended.'

I caught his eye in the rear view mirror and gave him a grateful smile as I drove, my hands shaking on the wheel, the windshield wipers working over-time. I followed the ambulance that now loomed in front, a sinister bright yellow, the rain driving down in long silver sheets as if we were in some kind of bad dream.

On reaching the hospital I screeched to a halt in the first parking space I saw. We jumped out of the car and rushed to the main entrance just as the ambulance pulled up at the massive open doors to the Accident and Emergency Department. Doctors and nurses, obviously alerted that there had been an incident of some kind rushed out and, lifting the stretcher carefully from the ambulance, carried it inside. We were too far away to see who was lying on the stretcher. We hurried in to the main reception area and told the receptionist, a kindly older lady with a soft, powdery face, who we were. She tutted at Becky's stifled sobs and fetched a blanket for her from the staff room as she was wet through and shivering.

'Oh, you poor girl,' she said warmly.

'All three of you, go and take a seat and I will bring you a warm drink. There's nothing that can be done at the moment. We've had no word from the doctor about the patient.'

She came back with hot chocolate and biscuits which Robbie and I ate and drank gratefully. Becky barely took a sip of the warm drink and not a crumb of the biscuits passed her lips.

She lay back in the chair now, her eyes closed and her face white and pinched. Robbie was pacing up and down, up and down, his trainers squeaking on the tiled floor.

Thoughts began to run around and around in my head. Where were Tom's parents? And his brother, Danny? Hadn't they been informed?

'Listen you two,' I said, 'I'm just going to have a word with that nice lady on reception, OK?'

Becky nodded listlessly and closed her eyes again.

Robbie said, 'Why, Mum? What's going on?'

'Please Robbie, look after Becky while I'm gone.' And when he made to come after me said forcefully, 'Robbie, please!'

Reluctantly he sat down next to his sister and crossing his arms over his chest grumbled, 'OK, but don't be long!'

I had a hunch and kept thinking of what the police officer had said. *There was no ID on him, he hasn't been identified yet.* Perhaps the bike had been stolen and Tom hadn't been riding it at all when the accident occurred. Surely that was worth looking into?

The receptionist was sitting at her desk looking at the screen of her computer as I approached her.

'Excuse me,' I said, 'But have you an ID yet for the young man that was brought in earlier? As far as we're aware, the motorbike involved in the accident belongs to a Tom Blatchford.'

'Yes — wait a minute. Mrs Masters, you said your name was, didn't you?'

'Yes, I'm Laurel Masters. Tom Blatchford is my daughter's boyfriend. We're all very worried about him.'

She gazed at the screen of her computer.

'I am sorry, Mrs Masters, but the motorbike has been identified as a Mr Thomas Blatchford's and his parents have been informed. I'm so sorry but we've still not heard of the extent of his injuries from the doctors. As soon as I hear anything I'll let you know.'

'Yes but is there ID for the rider of the bike? I mean, the bike might have been stolen.'

'I don't know, Mrs Masters, nothing has been said to me about that ... I think that if it wasn't Mr Blatchford, I would have been told by now.'

'Oh dear,' I said faintly, putting my hands to my mouth. 'Oh dear me ... ' I nodded to the receptionist, said, 'Thank you,' and began to walk away back to Becky and Robbie.

'Mrs Masters?' she called after me. 'You go and sit tight. I'll bring you some more hot chocolate. OK?'

'You're very kind,' I told her. 'Thank you.'

No sooner had I sat down under Robbie's interested and interrogating gaze than the receptionist came along with another tray of hot drinks and more biscuits. She placed a caring hand on my shoulder and gave me a warm understanding smile as she left the room. I gave Robbie a tight shake of my head as I sat forward reaching for my drink.

'Come on, Becky,' I said. 'Drink this, it will make you feel better.'

She shook her head. 'No, I just want Tom . . .'

I pulled her close and she sobbed again, her head on my shoulder, I fought back my own tears but they were there, threatening, just below the surface.

I supposed there was no doubt now that Tom had been riding the bike, but I still wasn't sure. I had a hunch, my brain was whirring thinking of possible scenarios.

Suddenly the door opened and a face appeared, a white tense face.

'Hello, I'm Mrs Blatchford, Irene . . . may I join you? Oh hello,

Becky . . . what are you doing here?'

Becky sat up straight away. 'Oh . . . Irene . . . I . . .'

Of course, I thought. *They wouldn't know that Becky saw Tom's bike at the scene of the crash. They wouldn't know how distraught she's been.*

Another face appeared, a man — Mr Blatchford I assumed — and then there was somebody else behind him.

I couldn't see who it was at first, there were so many tears blinding my eyes, but when I saw him run over to Becky and pull her to him, I knew that Tom was there with us in this very room and not in the operating theatre, his body being investigated for injuries by doctors and nurses, after being involved in an accident on his motorbike. My heart felt so light, I was surprised that it wasn't floating about in the very air above me.

But if Tom was here safe and sound, who had been on that bike tonight? Who was in the operating theatre right at this moment in time?

I had a feeling who it might be,

but really, as long as it wasn't Tom, was it my place to interfere?

Yes, I thought, *of course it is, Mr and Mrs Blatchford must have been informed that their son, Tom, was in the hospital. But as he was with them, they would know that it wasn't him on the bike that evening. So was it perhaps their other son, Danny?*

★ ★ ★

I waited a few days before going to the sanctuary to pick up the personal belongings I'd left there. I decided I would go on a Tuesday morning, as it was the only day when Puppy Love was open in the afternoon only. I knew that I could get all my stuff and be gone before Jack arrived.

I hadn't heard from him again — I assumed he was waiting until Friday when he was expecting me to appear at work begging for forgiveness with my tail between my legs just like one of his many dogs. Well, he would have to wait a long time for that.

I don't know why, call it another hunch, but I didn't drive into the car park at the sanctuary but parked on the main road at the top and walked down. Reaching the gates to Puppy Love, I went through and crunched my way across the car park to the office building.

It was raining again, a fine misty rain that hung in the air like a cloud, obscuring the beautiful view that I usually liked to sit and linger over. There was a chilly breeze making me hunch my shoulders to my ears as, using my key, I quietly let myself in and went straight to my desk.

Glancing around, I noticed that the office wasn't quite as tidy as I liked it to be. No doubt Paula had been there putting down her own rules and regulations for how she liked things to be, which definitely wasn't the same as mine.

Taking a carrier bag, I began to put my things into it, business diary, pencil case, pens, cuddly Puppy Love toy dog that Jack had given me to sit on my desk, note books, pictures of Alfie, Becky and Robbie, a calendar — it's amazing what you can accumulate, even at work! Especially at work, I suppose.

Suddenly and to my horror I heard a car pulling up outside and, rushing to the window and peering out, I saw a red mini with its private number plate ending in DEB.

Oh no, I thought. *Not Paula. Is this it then — is this the showdown?*

After a couple of minutes, Paula emerged from the driver's seat. She wore a long fur coat that she wrapped more tightly around herself with one hand as she ran towards the office in the driving misty rain. Watching her running, her head down, so heavy and ungainly, I wondered how I'd ever thought she could have been a model.

I went back to sit at my desk, my heart beating hard, ready for her when she walked through the door.

To my surprise, she went around the back of the building and entered through the door that led into the kitchen and the little room where the big, heavy safe was kept — the safe room, as Jack and

I always called it. I was able to see her through the window in the office door as she stepped inside and immediately got out her mobile phone.

'Hi, it's me . . . '

Unintelligible speech.

'It's Paula, you dolt! Surely you recognise my voice!'

I don't know why but straight away I got out my mobile phone and pressed the record button. While doing that I missed a bit of the conversation but the rest went like this . . .

'I know. What an idiot! He really thinks the baby is his . . . what a pushover!'

Unintelligible speech from the other end of the phone.

'I borrowed the baby from my friend, Donna . . . yes, she's called Leigh, not Jacqueline after him, and is four months old, not three as I told him.'

More speech from the other end.

'I'm going to borrow her again. I'll just show her to him every now and then — that should keep him happy.' She laughed, tinkly and silvery as a bell.

'OK, I'll go now then — '

Paula paused, listening intently.

'Yes, I'm going to do it now. I've got the code for the safe. He won't miss a few hundred here, a few hundred there . . . he's not without . . .'

Raucous speech from the other end. 'Oh, George, stop it . . . I'll do what I can.' Paula listened again.

'Yeah, see you soon. Ciao!'

'Ciao?' I thought shaking my head, bewildered, 'Why Italian?' Ah . . . maybe George was an Italian? Not a very Italian name though. I shrugged and shook my head. Maybe it was short for Giorgio or something like that.

She put the phone into her coat pocket and went into the safe room. I supposed I didn't really need to film it — she'd said it all on the phone, 'he won't miss a few hundred here, a few hundred there' — and anyway I wouldn't be able to, I'd give myself away if I opened the door I was peering through now and joined her in the safe room.

I could see her hunched over the safe,

like a big, lumbering bear in her furry coat. I heard the sound of the lock being turned and the heavy suck of the door as it opened and then the rustle of notes and the chink of coins.

My heart sank for Jack, for all his hard-earned money going into such greedy hands and for the shock that he would get when he found out that the baby wasn't his. I'd just known that I was right about that. Another hunch or what?

* * *

I waited until she'd finished her devious work and left the building, roaring away in her red Mini like Cruella de Vil. Then, hastily, I took my bag of belongings and headed out of the door, carefully putting the key into an envelope and posting it through the letter box. I heard it fall with a clatter to the floor. With a sinking heart, I walked away, regretting just a little that I hadn't left a goodbye note for Jack for in all probability I'd never see him again.

10

Becky was singing in the shower and it was like music to my ears, a balm to my heart and . . . I don't know . . . sunshine to my soul. Is that a saying? But you get my drift.

I was so happy that Becky was singing in the shower because it meant that everything was OK in her little part of the world. She was still seeing Tom and, if anything, they were closer than ever after the terrible shock of the accident.

'Oh, what a relief it was to know that it wasn't Tom who'd been hurt on that motorbike,' she told me. She shook her head slowly and sadly like a very old woman.

My hunch proved to be right — it was Danny Blatchford and not Tom who had been on the motorbike that evening. He'd stolen it from the garden where Tom had left it while he went into the house to get changed before going on to his evening job stacking shelves at Yarrows, the little supermarket in Cobby.

When Tom went outside and the bike wasn't there, he'd had a gut feeling that his brother had taken it and when the police rang to tell his mum and dad that he, Tom, had been identified as having been involved in an accident while he, Tom, was right there with them, they all guessed what had happened.

If Becky hadn't been walking home from Mandy's, she wouldn't have seen a thing and been none the wiser, but instead got caught up in an awful situation which, apart from Danny's injuries, had, thankfully, ended on a positive note. No, Danny wouldn't be going anywhere for a while, not with a broken leg (as Robbie predicted — 'Wow, have you got a crystal ball, Robbie?' Becky asked him) — and a broken pelvis both of which were going to take some time to heal. But they would heal so, overall, he was a lucky young man.

The wreckage that I'd seen when we drove past that night didn't bode well for whoever had been riding the bike and I was surprised that Danny Blatchford had even survived.

'What about the theft of your bike, though?' I heard Becky ask Tom, 'What are you going to do about that? Will you press charges?'

'No,' he replied, shaking his head. 'Danny must have learned his lesson from his injuries at least . . . perhaps it's a good thing that the accident happened and that from now on, he'll stay out of trouble! But no — ' he shook his head adamantly — 'I can't press charges against my brother.'

'But what about your bike?'

'I'm hoping I can claim on the insurance,' Tom assured her, 'Don't worry, everything will work out fine, Becky.'

Hmm, I thought wistfully, watching the two of them, both so young with so much to learn and so much to go through separately and as a couple. *If only I had one half of Tom's optimism, I'd be happy.*

I'd watched the incriminating film of Paula several times on my phone and was still undecided as to what I should do with it. It was probably best that I show Jack — at least he'd know for sure that she was still not to be trusted — but what would he think of me? Would he just assume that I was making trouble? Did he like living in a little bubble of a now very sweet Paula with a pretty baby that he thought was his? *Oh, what should I do? Would someone please tell me what to do?*

My phone vibrated in my pocket and taking it out, I saw with a sinking heart that it was a text from Jack.

Laurel, you haven't turned up for work today. I will only accept your letter of resignation if you give me one week's notice as per your contract. Thanks. J.

'Oh no,' I said to myself as, rushing upstairs, I searched frantically through the box where I kept all my important documents. Retrieving my contract of employment, I read it through, my eyes quickly scanning the words, when the sentence, *One week's notice must be given if employed for less than two years . . .* popped out at me.

Yes, unfortunately, he was right, it was there in black and white. I'd totally forgotten about working notice — maybe because I only went in one day a week? Oh well, I had no choice but to go in today and face the music. I'd make sure my phone was with me and, if I thought the time was right, I would show Jack the film that I'd made and see what he had to say to that.

* * *

Maggie, busily working in her garden as I went out to my car, rushed to the fence and said, 'Laurel, Kath said she'll put our boggy gardens on the agenda for the next full town council meeting which is two weeks yesterday. She said there's no point in it going to the planning committee and then being referred to council, so . . . '

I nodded. 'Yes that makes sense.'

'That's a Thursday, Laurel. Will you be available to come along?'

'Oh yes, of course,' I told her, 'How

about Paul Timpson? Any word from him?'

'Not yet.' She gave a wry twist of her mouth. 'I don't blame him really, you know, Laurel, if he doesn't speak on our behalf. I've been thinking about his situation and he's right, he would be stirring up a hornet's nest. What do you think?'

'Yes, I feel a bit sorry for him to tell you the truth. He's caught between a rock and a hard place as they say.'

'You're right, he is. We'll just have to tell them at council that it was common knowledge that the area was green belt and there was talk of a flood plain with, of course, no mention of names. We'll quote what was in the papers. The builders are so much at fault — they must have known while building, or even before, that the land wasn't suitable!'

I drove away feeling slightly apprehensive already at having to stand up in council and speak, but if it had to be done, then I would do it as a support for Maggie. And as she always said, 'It's our right to fight!' She was a one for campaigning, was Maggie.

I arrived at the sanctuary far too soon; I wasn't prepared. My heart was hammering and my mouth felt dry as a bone.

Jerking backwards and forwards as I drove over the stony car park, I pulled into a parking spot and gazed at the view in front of me. It was a far better day with no misty rain to obscure the beautiful vista and I immediately felt peaceful and quiet, all my anxious rage from this morning quite gone. The air was full of the high-pitched mewling of cats and the occasional woof of a dog which made me think of Alfie and the run that I was planning to go on with him when I got home.

A lot of people were milling around the entrance to the office building, some carrying cute kittens and a couple with dogs on leads. I spied Jack inside running backwards and forwards, but no sign of the delectable Paula. Scanning the car park I could see no sign of her little red Mini either. The relief I felt was indescribable and I felt quite buoyant as I entered the office and put my bag on my empty desk and took off my coat and hung it neatly on the coat stand.

Jack turned around from where he sat at the computer.

'Ah, Laurel,' he gave me his lovely Hollywood mega-watt smile. 'Thanks so much for coming in. Please could you deal with Corrine and Lee over there? They're about to adopt the little black kitten, Suki.'

'Yes of course,' I said, rushing over to the happy couple, who were holding on carefully to a tiny black ball of fluff who purred with contentment in the crook of Corinne's arms.

The day was over in a flash with still no sign of Paula, which was brilliant. It was really just like old times. I felt as if a weight had been lifted from my shoulders. Jack turned the pretty Puppy Love sign on the door from Open to Closed, and we began to pack up and get ready for home.

'Laurel,' Jack said, just as I was

buttoning up my coat and gathering up my hat and gloves. 'It's been so busy today that I haven't had a chance to speak to you before …'

'Well, whatever you're going to say, Jack, the answer is no! I'm leaving now, and I'm not coming back. I've worked my notice.'

He gave a wry smile. 'I wasn't going to ask you anything just yet,' he explained. 'I wanted to tell you that money has gone missing from the safe.'

My heart started to thump very strongly and, my legs suddenly felt so weak and wobbly that I had to sit down. I put a hand to my chest and took a deep breath. Jack crouched down in front of me and took my hands, hands that had suddenly gone ice cold, and clasped them in his warm ones.

'I'm not accusing you, Laurel … I know you wouldn't do that. I know you wouldn't steal.'

'Well, who would, then?' I looked him straight in the eye.

'There's only one other person that's

been working here, isn't there?'

I nodded, yes, wishing that I didn't find him so attractive, wishing that my heart didn't rev up a beat every time he was near me and wishing that I could take my eyes away from the slice of hairy chest that showed at the neck of his shirt.

'That person hasn't been averse to stealing from me before, as you well know, Laurel. If you know anything, please tell me.'

I thought of the film on my phone. Yes, there was proof of Paula stealing — but also all the derogatory comments about him and information about the baby. Did Jack want to hear that too?

I was so torn. Should I or shouldn't I tell him?

What a dilemma!

I pulled my hands away from his grip and stood up. I needed to walk around. I needed to think.

Then all of a sudden I knew what I should do and I began to gabble. Jack stopped me, saying, 'Calm down, Laurel, please . . . just take it easy.' and then

I slowed down and began to speak slowly and carefully as I told him everything.

'May I see the film please, Laurel?' he asked. I put my phone on the desk and pressed the button to play. The film began and there she was, Paula, in all her glory, a hard-hearted witch wearing a long fur coat, mobile phone to her ear, and that tinkling laugh of hers sending shivers down my spine.

Jack listened to it all, his face impassive, unflinching, as awful words about how she'd used a four-month-old baby to hoodwink him spewed from her pretty mouth.

It was so obvious that this was a ploy to get close to him again so that she could steal his money, so that she could use him again to get what she wanted. There was no baby for Jack, it was all lies. The look of despair on his face broke my heart.

'I can't believe she lied about the baby.' He shook his head over and over again. 'And to show me a baby, her friend's child, and say it was mine . . . well, that's just cruel! The money she stole from me doesn't seem to matter so much against that.'

I stayed silent. I didn't know what to say, but I put my hand firmly on his and squeezed it reassuringly.

'Stay, Laurel,' he said softly. 'Please stay? You've been so good for me. I've been happier with you in my life than I've been for a long time.'

And when I didn't reply, he said, 'I just won't accept your resignation . . . I won't, I mean it.'

'On one condition,' I told him slowly.

'Anything!'

'I can't work here if Paula is here as well. She is rude and obnoxious to me and I can't work in that atmosphere.'

'That's no problem' he said. 'I'm going to tell her to go. After this, I could never trust her again.'

'I'm surprised you let her back into your life,' I said. 'After what she did before.'

'It was the baby, Laurel, I thought I was a father. I believed her. If it wasn't for that, she would have been gone long before. So you'll stay?'

'Yes.' I nodded.

'Fantastic!' crowed Jack, his blue eyes shining. Why did he have to be such a gorgeous-looking man? 'I'd like to take you for a drink, Madam,' he said while executing a courtly bow — just as he'd done when we first came to the sanctuary to choose Alfie, our wonder dog, and take him home.

I gave a small smile.

'No, I'm not ready for that yet, Jack. I'm afraid I may be tempted to walk out on you without drinking my wine as I did before. I'll see you here next Friday and we'll see how it goes, OK?'

'Yes,' he said. 'I knew better than to go after you when you walked out of the Star pub. Am I on trial now?'

'Yes, I think you are,' I said as I made to head out of the door. 'After a month, I shall give you marks out of ten.'

Jack stood there, a sexy little smile hovering around his luscious lips.

'A month? Surely not that long?'

'A month,' I said firmly.

'Oh, you are a tyrant, Laurel! But you are probably quite right. After a month I hope to achieve a ten out of ten! And I quote, 'A gem cannot be polished without friction, nor a man perfected without trials.''

He gave another little bow as, shaking my head at him, I opened the door and let it close softly behind me.

11

The council chamber was busy and full of chatter when Maggie and I walked in on that Thursday evening, my heart fluttering as if a bird was in there flapping its wings and desperately trying to get out.

I'd spent a strange sleepless night with all sorts of things running around and around in my mind, particularly Jack, and his far too handsome face which kept appearing in front of me, his beautiful lips pouting and ready to be kissed.

I felt hot and bothered at even thinking about him and I got a sudden surge of heat that went right through my body.

Maggie must have noticed for she gave me a strange look and said, 'Are you OK, Laurel?'

I nodded and gave her a small smile.

'Don't be nervous,' she whispered. 'We'll just tell it as it is, OK?' I noticed that Maggie had curled her hair for the occasion and wore a lovely bright red lipstick.

I nodded and glanced around the room, noticing that one of the tables, covered with a beautiful cloth, was set out with sandwiches and cake and that a tea trolley stood in the corner laden with cups and saucers, a flask of hot water and coffee and tea.

The chamber itself was very impressive with its lovely dark panelled walls, pictures of all the Mayors from the 1970s through to the present day displayed on them. The panels looked well polished and dusted and the air smelled of beeswax as well as an underlying odour of old damp buildings and cellars. I could hear voices from the balcony and, even when straining my neck to look up, I couldn't see who was there.

'Members of the public are able to sit up there and watch the show,' Maggie told me with a playful wink.

We moved across to the food table to help ourselves to a warm drink and a sandwich, passing closely by Kath who was in deep conversation with the Mayor.

'Ah, Councillor Gates,' said a tall,

rather distinguished-looking man who I noticed wore a badge stating that he was Councillor Williams. He'd been Mayor twice, by the look of two other badges that he wore. He took a sip of his insipid-looking tea.

'Councillor Williams,' said Maggie. 'How nice to see you. This is my friend and neighbour, Laurel Masters.'

'Come to talk about your boggy gardens, have you?' said another voice and a rather large man came to stand with us. He was broad and powerful-looking with 'hands like shovels' as my mum would have remarked. He also wore a Previous Mayor badge.

'Councillor Rawdon. Yes, we have. This is my friend and neighbour, Laurel Masters. Laurel, Councillor Williams and Councillor Rawdon . . .'

Councillor Rawdon enclosed my hand in a vice-like grip as I nodded hello. We chatted about this and that until a Councillor Melrose also came over to discuss boggy gardens which he, for some reason, seemed to find hilarious. He also did a passable impersonation of Eric More-cambe which made everyone giggle.

Kath gave us a little wave from her seat next to the Mayor but she was obviously too busy to come over and talk to us, as several councillors were milling around asking questions and waving pieces of paper.

I noticed Maggie gazing searchingly around the room.

'What is it? I asked, 'Still hoping that Paul Timpson will turn up?' I took a last swig of coffee, the strong tasting dregs making me grimace, before placing the cup and saucer on the table.

'Yes — I did think he might change his mind but . . . '

'We can't blame him though can we, Maggie? I'd keep out of it if it was me — as I'm sure you would.'

'Yes, you're quite right.' Then, consulting her watch Maggie said, 'The Mayor, Councillor Iqbal, will be banging his gavel at any minute, Laurel, so I'll have to sit over there with the other Councillors. You'll be OK to sit here.'

She indicated a space next to a thin young man who had a pad in front of him the top of the page covered with various shorthand squiggles. He clutched a pen as if he was ready and waiting. I assumed he was from the local Cobby News so gave him a smile as I sat down, picking up a copy of the agenda. I noticed that Maggie and I were to speak just after the update from the planning committee which I suppose made really good sense.

'Good evening, councillors and guests,' intoned Councillor Iqbal as the clock struck six o'clock. 'Welcome to our full Town Council meeting . . . please let us begin.'

He banged the gavel and the meeting commenced. There were various formalities such as approving the previous minutes. A Councillor Webster stood up to talk about the events and leisure committee and their plans for events for the following few months, which I must say sounded very exciting. I knew that Maggie helped to organise the events and I envied her that.

Councillors Holmes stood to give an update on planning issues. I sat barely listening to him talking about the amount of planning applications that had come in recently and a few contentious issues that the committee were working through, knowing that at any minute Maggie and I would have to get up in front of all the people sitting in the chamber.

My heart thumped and my mouth felt dry, not helped probably by the coffee that I'd just drunk. In my panic and my mind being so far away from everything that was happening, Councillor Iqbal's words took some time to penetrate, as he said,' And now, Councillors, we have a guest tonight — a Mrs Laurel Masters who will speak with Councillor Gates on the subject of their boggy gardens.'

There was a general swell of laughter as Maggie and I rose from our seats and walked to the front of the chamber close to where the Mayor and Kath were sitting.

I was aware of many pairs of eyes

upon us as first of all Maggie began to speak. We told them where we lived, the notorious White Church Lane development. We had barely got started before Councillor Holmes stood up — without permission from the Mayor — and said, 'I was always against that development being built. It was well known from the outset that the land was both green belt and a flood plain!'

'Hear hear,' said a good half of the councillors while the Mayor banged his gavel hard and said, 'Councillor Holmes, please sit down and allow our guest Mrs Masters and Councillor Gates to speak. Councillors will be permitted to speak at the end . . . with my permission only!'

There was a short silence where Councillor Holmes huffily plonked himself down in his seat, before Maggie carried on saying, 'Yes — you are quite right, Councillor Holmes. The land was known to be green belt and a flood plain and we can only wonder why the application was allowed to go ahead.'

'From what we have been told,' I said,

my voice quavering slightly as I took over from Maggie, 'it was advised that the application not go ahead by a person in the planning department. This advice was ignored and the application was put forward again by somebody else and allowed to proceed.' We carried on with our speech until Maggie wrapped it up by saying, 'The builders were well aware when they bought the land that it was unsuitable and we are now left with boggy, unusable gardens. We would appreciate advice on how to proceed.'

A Councillor Smith stood up, a young man with a smooth, unlined baby face and curly hair like a 1970s perm.

'For God's sake, ladies, all I can say is that you shouldn't have bought a house on that development if you knew what had been said about the land. Common sense isn't it?'

Maggie and I exchanged outraged glances and Maggie retaliated by saying, 'We learned that information only after we had moved in, Councillor!'

'Well . . . you should have moved back

out then shouldn't you?' he retorted.

'I like it there,' said Maggie stoutly.

'Well, put up with your boggy garden then,' he retorted.

There was much laughter and talking which the Mayor brought under control by banging the gavel so hard that poor Kath sitting next to him almost jumped out of her skin. I almost expected to see her skin draped like a coat over the back of her chair.

There were many more comments made by the Councillors about our speech, some for and some against. We answered questions and in the lull which followed, Councillor Iqbal declared that this matter should be brought again to the next full town council meeting as they were no nearer at this meeting to solving the problem. An invitation would be sent to a planning officer from Skelmanthorpe District and also a representative from the Environment Agency, as well as the foreman of the builders, Cobby Developments. He asked Maggie and myself if we were happy with that and we said that we were.

'Thank you for coming and speaking, Mrs Masters. You may stay for the rest of the meeting if you wish, but you, Councillor Gates,' and here he gave a broad smile, 'have no choice but to stay, so please take your seat.'

He gave a slight bow of his head and to uproarious applause Maggie and I thanked the council for giving us the opportunity to speak and walked away.

I mouthed to Maggie, 'I'll go on the balcony,' and pointed up with a finger. She nodded and gave me a thumbs-up sign.

What an enjoyable session, I thought, as I climbed the tiny stone steps to the balcony. *And what a varied response.* I giggled to myself at the rudeness of some of the councillors, but how exciting being on council was. I really did envy Maggie her part in it all.

There were so many thoughts jostling around in my head that I wasn't prepared for who I saw as I entered the balcony. Two heads turned at the creak of the door, one belonging to Paul Timpson who gave me a very charming smile and the other, making my heart beat even harder than ever, I saw belonged to Jack.

Baby blues glowing, he said, 'Hello, Laurel, you did really well down there. I was so proud of you.'

* * *

Maggie met me at the bottom of the steep stone steps from the balcony as I clattered down with Jack and Paul Timpson following hard on my heels.

Catching sight of me, she said, 'Do you fancy a drink, Laurel? The Star, I thought?'

My heart sank at the thought of The Star pub, the place where Jack and I had met only recently and where I'd walked out and left him. We'd barely exchanged a word on the balcony after Jack's greeting, apart from hello, but after all what could we have said in the presence of Paul Timpson?

Before I could say anything she said,

'Oh hello, Paul and . . . well, hello,' as she saw Jack.

Paul Timpson nodded and returned her greeting. I watched as he peered through the Council Chamber door obviously hoping to catch sight of Kath.

'Um, this is Jack Garthwaite,' I said introducing him to Maggie. 'He's the owner of Puppy Love Dog and Cat Sanctuary. I work there on a Friday.'

'Oh, how do you do.' She held out her hand and Jack gripped it saying how nice it was to meet her.

My heart sank as, walking down the stairs to the front door, Maggie continued, 'Oh, Mr Garthwaite, you must come for a drink with us.'

'Jack — please call me Jack. Well, that's very kind of you, um, Councillor — ?'

'Gates,' she said, 'But call me Maggie.'
'Laurel, is that OK with you? If I come for a drink?'

Stuck for what to say without appearing rude I said tightly, 'Of course,' as we stepped outside into the cold frosty air. It was a clear night, a velvety black sky sprinkled with stars arching overhead. The moon hung motionless and very low, like a great, glaring white face. Stephen Gates was there, smoking a cigarette which he hastily stubbed out as Maggie went over to him and hooked her arm through his.

'This is my husband, Stephen,' she said to Jack. 'Stephen you obviously know Laurel but this is a friend of hers, Jack Garthwaite.'

'Pleased to meet you, Jack,' said Stephen holding out his hand and shaking Jack's forcefully.

'Good meeting?' he asked.

'Not bad,' replied Maggie. 'We'll tell you all about it won't we, Laurel?'

I nodded and Stephen, rubbing his hands together, said, 'Are we off to the pub then?' He directed his gaze to Maggie but smiled around and said, 'Laurel, Jack, you joining us?'

'Yes, of course,' I said lightly. I was aware of Jack staring hopefully at me but I just couldn't meet his gaze. If I did, I had a hunch (another hunch?) that I'd be lost, despite matters not being at all right between us at the moment.

'Can we wait for Kath and Paul?' asked Maggie. 'Hopefully they'll join us.'

The doors opened and a surge of people came out, mainly councillors laughing and joking amongst themselves, followed by Kath who was buttoning up her coat and pulling the belt tightly around her slender waist. Paul followed close behind.

'Good night, councillors,' she said. 'See you tomorrow.'

'Yes see you tomorrow, Kath,' growled Councillor Rawdon as he lumbered away with Councillor Williams and Councillor Melrose who, while waving to Kath, was doing a funny thing with his glasses to make them all laugh.

★ ★ ★

The Star pub, familiar to me now, was warm and cosy, a fire roaring in the wood burning stove, and fairly busy for a Thursday evening. However Paul pointed out a table for six and the three of us went to grab it while the men went to the bar.

We'd barely sat down before Maggie said, 'Well, Laurel, really, I didn't know you had it in you! What a gorgeous man!'

'Yes,' said Kath dreamily. 'He looks like a hero from a romantic novel . . . I mean, he really does.'

I smiled. 'I met him at the sanctuary when I adopted Alfie.'

'Well, lucky you.'

'What?' I said impishly. 'For Alfie or Jack?'

They both smiled and said, 'For both of course!'

Hmm, I thought. *What would they think if they knew the situation between us at the moment?*

I was quite annoyed with Jack really for turning up tonight, especially after what had happened between us only last week. To be frank, at the moment, I didn't see a future for us at all, not any more, and I definitely didn't think that he would get a ten out of ten from me in a month's time.

Had my feelings changed because of Paula? I wasn't sure.

Nevertheless I said quite happily, 'I think you two ladies are very lucky too — after all, Stephen and Paul are both very attractive men.'

The men came back then with the drinks, chatting and looking rather pleased with themselves, foaming pints and glasses of wine in their hands. Jack sat down next to me and gave me a large glass of red wine, saying 'Cheers' as he did so.

We chatted around the table, all six of us, discussing the meeting and shredding some of the councillors to bits, especially Councillor Smith, the young man with the smooth face and curly hair who had been very rude to myself and Maggie.

'Oh, take no notice,' said Maggie disdainfully, 'I have problems with him all the time. Some of the councillors think they're better than anyone else!'

'Yes,' agreed Kath. 'The gold in amongst the dross are people who do so much good work, like Councillor Rawdon and Councillor Melrose. Councillor Williams too . . . they're all on the council for the right reasons. And whatever might be said about Councillor Holmes, he knows a lot about planning.'

'So that sort of makes up for it?' said Paul with a grin. He went on to talk about our boggy gardens and apologised again for not speaking up for us.

'No worries, Paul,' Maggie said. 'We understand totally, don't we Laurel?'

'Of course,' I said, and Jack butted in, 'I think they did extremely well tonight, don't you, Paul?'

'Yes I do. A very good speech, stating the facts, asking for advice, but apportioning no blame. Very good work, ladies.'

Kath asked Maggie a question and Paul said something to Stephen which started separate conversations. Jack turned to me and whispered, 'Laurel, I haven't been able to get in touch with Paula as yet. I've sent her a few texts asking her to ring me so we can get all the truths out, about the money and the baby.'

'Hmm, well good luck with that Jack,' I said, and then with a frown, I added, 'So you haven't heard back from her for almost a week?'

He shook his head and took a sip of beer. The foam stuck to his lip which he licked off with the tip of his tongue sending a shiver down my spine. OK, however the situation was between us, he was still a very attractive man.

'Is that usual?' I asked.

'Well, not since she reappeared,' he said. 'I found that she was in touch just a bit too much if anything.'

Glancing around to make sure that the others weren't listening I whispered urgently, 'Actually Jack, you shouldn't have turned up tonight . . . you know what I said last time we spoke. I didn't want to go for a drink with you yet. We agreed on a month, remember?'

'But you said that it was OK if I came with you . . . when Maggie asked.'

'Yes — but I didn't mean it!' I hissed.

'Oh,' he said seemingly puzzled but then, shamefaced, said, 'I just wanted to wish you well for your speech.'

'A text message would have been enough,' I interrupted.

'I wanted to see you, Laurel.' And after a brief silence he said carefully, 'Even if the baby was mine, it isn't Paula that I want. I haven't wanted her for a long time.'

We gazed at each other, brown eyes meeting blue, as he breathed softly, 'It's you I want, Laurel . . . only you.'

I opened my mouth to say something — I wasn't sure what — but Stephen raising his glass with a smile said, 'Another drink everyone?'

There was a general yes and nods all around, so all three men went to the bar again.

I watched Jack as he walked away, my heart thumping almost up into my mouth. Maggie, Kath and I began to talk amongst ourselves.

Suddenly we heard raised voices coming from the bar area and then the smashing of a glass and within seconds the whole pub had erupted. People began to stand up, all clapping and cheering, necks straining over the crowds, trying to see what was going on.

I could just about see Jack, amongst all the people, standing near the bar, a woman with short blonde hair close by him. My heart sank right into my smart black shoes. It was her — Paula — a sneer on her face and her arm raised as if to hit someone.

I lowered my head, even though I knew full well that she wouldn't be able to see me, but making myself look as small as possible could only be a good thing in the circumstances. What was wrong with her? She must have problems if she thought that confronting Jack in such a public place was a good idea.

I saw Jack put his hand on the small of her back and steer her outside, as all the while she tried to hang back glaring over her shoulder.

Eventually, the door swung closed behind them and, as if on cue, there was a whirr and a click from the jukebox and Elton John began to sing, '*Saturday night's all right for fighting, Saturday night's all right, all right, all right . . .'*

'I don't know about Saturday night,' I heard somebody say with a grim chuckle. 'But Thursday night definitely is.'

12

Waking up this morning in the cold dark dawn, my mouth dry and my stomach in knots, a tight sickly pain across my forehead, I knew that I really didn't want to face work — or Jack, come to that — today.

But to ring in sick and leave him working alone when Puppy Love was such a busy place was out of the question. I recalled the sympathetic glances from Kath and Maggie as they watched Jack leave the pub with Paula, and felt ill all over again. How would I be able to face any of them now? What must they have thought when they saw Jack walk out and leave me in the pub so as to make sure his ex-girlfriend got home safely?

I closed my eyes seeing last night played out like a scene from a film, like some sort of tawdry western in a saloon bar where the girl confronted her man and stole him away.

No, surely not, Jack had said that he wanted me and not her . . . but was that true?

'Laurel, are you OK?' Maggie had asked, putting a comforting arm around my shoulders as I stood rigid, suppressed tears burning at the back of my eyes. Kath said nothing but I felt her small hand creep into mine and give a caring squeeze.

'Good God,' said Stephen, when he came back to the table carrying drinks on a tray, closely followed by Paul. 'Do you know her, Laurel?'

'Yes, I do . . . she's Jack's ex, Paula Lee, just recently come back to claim him again. Where's Jack? Should I go to him?'

I started to take my coat from the back of the chair, and picked up my hat and gloves.

'No, that's probably not a good idea,' said Paul hastily. 'Jack flagged down a passing taxi and said he'd see her home.'

'Wow, what a piece of work,' said Stephen.

Paul nodded emphatically at Stephen and said with raised eyebrows, 'She certainly is!' And then he turned to me. 'Jack said he's sorry, Laurel, but he'll be in touch tomorrow.'

'Did she hit him with a glass?' I asked Paul and Stephen.

'She tried to, but we took it away from her. Outside the pub she was like a wild cat!'

'Here,' said Kath, putting a drink in front of me. 'Have another wine and then we'll go home . . . OK?'

A little tap at the door brought me out of my reverie and a voice said, 'Mum, can I come in?'

Quickly wiping at my eyes with the tips of my fingers I said, 'Yes, of course, Becky, come in, love . . . '

My daughter entered the room carrying a tray bearing a mug of steaming coffee and some buttered toast, Alfie following close at her heels. He jumped up onto the bed and snuggled down beside me.

Becky and Tom had still been up when

I'd got in last night, waiting for me so that I could tell them how the speech for the full town council had gone. Of course I'd told them all that had happened after that in the pub too.

'Mum,' she said decisively, as she helped me to sit up, putting a pillow at my back, and gently placing the tray across my knee. I took a comforting sip of coffee as she carried on speaking. 'You're to stay here today. Tom and I will go to the sanctuary to give the Hollywood man a helping hand.'

'But Becky . . . you . . . won't . . . '

'We will know what to do, and it's only for today anyway, so you stay put. You don't look well and would probably have had to ring in sick. Robbie will be here if you need anything. Oh, and Tom and I are going to the hospital to see Danny tonight, so we'll go straight there from the sanctuary.'

'You're going to see Danny? But that's wonderful.' Tears threatened again and my lips wobbled as I tried to bite into the toast that Becky had so kindly made me.

'Yes — he's a lot nicer than I thought, Mum, certainly not the ogre he's made out to be. You must meet him when he's better.'

'Yes, I'd like that . . . and thank you for this, Becky,' I said, indicating the breakfast. 'Remember to tell Jack, won't you, that I'm not feeling well.'

'Don't worry, Mum, we'll tell him. And if you don't feel like walking Alfie later, Robbie will.'

'I'll walk Alfie,' I told her. 'I'm sure I'll feel like some exercise later!'

She gave me a quick kiss on the forehead and disappeared out of the door — content, I think, that like a good nurse she'd left her patient with an easy mind.

Putting the tray down on the floor beside the bed, I snuggled back down into the pillows — just for a couple more minutes, I thought, while the coffee did its work. My eyelids felt deliciously heavy, and accompanied by Alfie's gentle breathing I promptly fell asleep.

★ ★ ★

I awoke with a jolt later — much later, as I saw from my phone, where the time shone an accusing bright green. I'd been asleep for six hours! Six hours? Hard to believe but, well, I must have needed it.

The warm, comforting presence of Alfie was no longer there so I assumed that Robbie must have taken him for a walk, although why Robbie wasn't at school I had no idea! I hoped he hadn't stayed away specifically because of me.

Peering harder at my phone in the dim bedroom, I saw that I had a little flashing message icon and clicked on it straight away. It was from Jack.

Laurel, I am so sorry for last night. Will tell you all when I see you. Please forgive me but I had no choice. Thank you for the help sent today, Becky and Tom were brilliant. That young man is made to work with animals. Both a total Godsend! Get well soon. Jx

Tears threatened again and I despised myself for being such a soft weak woman.

Flinging back the duvet, I got out of bed and, shrugging on my dressing gown, feet finding my slippers, I went downstairs, my phone clamped in my hand.

Other messages popped up too as I sat at the kitchen table drinking another cup of coffee, so hot that it scalded my tongue. These were from Maggie and from Kath, asking if I was OK and wanting to know if I needed anything and showing an opinion of Jack that was very high.

Was this just because of his good looks and charm? His Hollywood aura? Before Paula came on the scene, I'd never doubted him, but now? I wasn't so sure.

It seems to me, Laurel, that Jack is a good man and none of last night was his fault. (from Maggie)

Laurel, I sympathise totally with Jack. I know I don't know the full story but I hope you will forgive him. (from Kath)

Yes, I thought, *it's all very well Maggie and Kath telling me to forgive him — but if all the time Paula is going to be around and stalking Jack, then the situation is no good for me.*

I really felt now that I should wash my hands of the whole thing and leave Jack and Paula to their own devices. I mean, look at me today, a bundle of nerves. I'd missed work and slept for hours and I wasn't even ill. That wasn't me — and it wasn't going to be me either, that's for sure!

Robbie suddenly came bursting through the door followed by a very excited Alfie who ran up to me and put his head in my lap as if he hadn't seen me for years. I stroked his shiny fur, wet through from the rain.

'Woah, Mum,' said Robbie. 'You feeling OK now?' He looked flushed and happy, his coat open and almost off his shoulders, showing a wrinkled T-shirt and slightly soiled jeans. His boots were caked with mud, 'We've had a great walk, haven't we, Alfie?'

'Yes I'm fine,' I said as I took another sip of coffee, 'Thanks for taking Alfie out Robbie, but why aren't you in school?'

Gently pushing Alfie to one side, I stood up and fetched his special towel and began giving him a good rub down. He squirmed happily beneath my touch, his tail wagging crazily.

'Teacher training day, Mum.'

'Oh — OK.' A bit convenient that it was today, I thought.

He took off his boots and then his coat, putting it in a crumpled heap on the table.

'Robbie . . . coat!'

Pouting a bit, he went into the hallway to hang it up, talking all the time.

'I'll tell you what, Mum, guess who I saw on our walk?'

'Who?' I asked, letting Alfie go and searching in the cupboard for his treats. Yeah, Alfie's such a good boy.

'Dad and Mrs Fletcher . . . walking through the woods they were and guess what?'

Looking up from feeding Alfie his treats I said impatiently, 'What?' Conversation with Robbie was often a total guessing game.

'Dad said that me and Becky should go round to his place when Mrs Fletcher's there so we can meet properly.'

'Oh, that's great, Robbie. You must mention it to Becky when she gets home.'

'Yeah, I will . . . and guess what, Mum?'

'What?' I said yet again.

He was filling up the kettle now, splashing water all over the draining board and the floor.

'What I want to know is . . . why wasn't Mrs Fletcher at the teacher training day? Hmm? Skiving with Dad, was she?'

'Oh Robbie, you are funny,' I said, shaking my head as I went behind him with the dish cloth mopping up all the spilled water.

He gave his high pitched childish giggle and said brightly, 'Do you want a coffee, Mum?'

I nodded yes please.

Robbie repeated, 'And guess what, Mum?' as he spooned coffee and sugar into mugs.

'Robbie! What now? Just tell me, please.'

He glanced over his shoulder.

'Her name's Liz, not Mrs Fletcher. Well, it is Mrs Fletcher but Dad said we're to call her Liz.'

'That's nice.'

'Yeah, Liz is OK . . . as a name,' he said thoughtfully. 'But I think Laurel is better.'

He gave me my coffee and we chinked mugs, 'Liz or Elizabeth means Oath of God,' I told him. 'And Laurel means Laurel Tree. Does that make any difference?'

'No.' Vehemently Robbie shook his head, and then after a little pause, and a sip of his drink, he said again, 'Guess what, Mum?'

'Wha-aat?' I said, for the, what? Hundredth time?

'Yours is still the best!'

* * *

Alfie was sitting back on his haunches, tail wagging frantically, avidly watching me with his deep brown eyes as I searched through my drawer of running gear looking for a specific black top. I'd found the blue running skirt which lay on the bed like a piece of fallen summer sky, but now wanted the black top.

I glanced at him, tongue lolling like a smile from his mouth, yes — he knew what I was doing. He knew very well that I was getting ready for a run; he'd spied my trainers waiting patiently in the hallway, and of course he knew that he would be going with me. What a clever dog he was.

'Aah, look Alfie,' I said, waving the black top at him. 'I've found it.' He stood up, tail wagging even harder and began a sort of high pitched mewling as if to say, 'Hurry up hooman, I can't wait much longer, I need to be outside in the fresh air and smelling all sorts of wonderful things in the bushes and the woods as I run.'

'Come on, boy,' I said, checking that I'd got my phone and key. We were ready to leave the house. Becky was out on a walk with Tom, and Robbie with Ash, no doubt battling as friend and foe on computer games. It wasn't my Saturday for the hairdresser's, so Alfie and I were alone and free to go on a good long run. After the trauma of the past couple of days, I was determined to put everything out of my mind, including Jack and the awful Paula Lee. I wanted to clear my mind of her nastiness and feel clean again.

We set off running through our estate, the notorious White Church Lane, past all the identical houses with their small squares of garden and onto the main road into Cobby town centre. I'd decided we'd go to Cobby Cairn. I wanted to see if I had the strength to run up the steep grassy hill to the trig point right at the very top, as I did a few weeks ago.

'Cobby Cairn?' I asked Alfie as he ran, a speeding black blur at my side.

'Woof, woof, anywhere hooman,' is his reply as we sped along, past Cobby Cuts and Curls where all the girls and customers stared wide-eyed as we streaked past with a cheery wave.

Bloomers the baker came into view, its long queue straggling over the pavement.

'Go on love, go for it,' said a couple of jibing male voices. A few little kids started to run alongside for fun, their little faces red and their mothers shouting, 'Oi, Daisy, Jordan, get back here now!'

It was a Saturday and the towpath was busy. We had to dodge in and out of bikers tinkling their bells, and family groups walking as slowly as snails, flat-footed geese hissing and spitting and graceful swans fluttering their snowy feathers and parading proudly as catwalk models.

The canal was as black as the sky and so still, with barely a ripple, dotted with speckled ducks that honked and chattered like a crowd at a football match. The last of the leaves, golden and crimson, twirled slowly from the trees to float on the water like tiny baby boats.

I watched the blur of Alfie in front of me as I climbed the rutted track from the towpath, stumbling on tiny stones and slipping and sliding on the wet earth, the muscles in my legs tightening as I pulled myself up further and further onto the long flat stretch before the next climb up onto Cobby Cairn.

I could see the trig point from here lit up in a silvery glow as a sudden shaft of sunlight burst its way through the black forbidding clouds. With my breath rasping in my ears and in my head, filling my whole body it seemed, my heart thumping hard, I pulled myself up and up, stomach muscles clenching, until with a sigh of relief, I reached out and touched the cool damp stones of the cairn with the very tips of my fingers.

Standing at the top, Alfie beside me, my heart still pounding, I gazed out over the magnificent view of green fields and the straggling dry stone walls that divided them, and the trees, almost bare now with just a flash here and there of crimson, yellow and orange.

The wind was wilder up here and pulled at my hair like strong fingers, lifting it from my scalp and the back of my neck. *How lucky I am*, I thought. *To live here and be able to look at this beautiful view every day if I want to.* In the grand scheme of things, my boggy garden didn't seem to matter any more.

Alfie panted heavily, his tongue lolling from his mouth as if from a discarded shoe.

'You look like a pair of trainers with their tongues hanging out, Alfie,' I told him. 'A pair of running trainers, of course.'

'Woof,' he said, not a care in the world. *What's wrong with that hooman?* said his expression.

Slowly then, we left the trig and gathering my strength, wanting to preserve this feeling of wellbeing, thinking of all those lovely endorphins rushing about in my brain, I began to jog on the spot ready for the long run down.

Alfie was sniffing in the bushes, his long nose hidden in the greenery, tail wagging madly.

'Come on, boy,' I said, and began to walk fast, not wanting to get too cold, looking back every now and then to see if he'd moved yet and was following me. But no, he hadn't, he was still sniffing avidly, his tail moving even faster.

'Alfie!'

He was normally such an obedient

dog!

He looked at me and barked, sniffed again, looked up and barked, sniffed again . . . Curious, and yeah, just a little bit annoyed, I walked back to him. He barked harder the nearer I got and only stopped when I was right beside him, peering into the greenery, my hands parting the tiny branches and leaves and oh my God, what did I see? I couldn't believe my eyes.

Alfie was going crazy, jumping up and down and wriggling his supple body, his tail going like a pendulum on a very fast-moving clock and his tongue hanging out longer than ever.

'Wow, you are a clever boy,' I said to him, 'What have you found eh?'

He pushed his nose back into the bushes and began to lick the tiny, squirming bodies of six — oh no, there's another one, a tiny one, seven — abandoned puppies. Close to tears, my hands shaking and covering my mouth, I simply stared at them. They were just there in the bushes on the cold, hard ground.

Who could have done this? Who could be so cruel? They didn't even put them in a box or wrap them in a blanket! There was nothing to keep them warm, and no food, no drink. All they had was each other's body heat and, if I got much colder as surely I would, I might have to join them in their little tumbled heap.

Jack, I thought immediately. I'm going to have to contact Jack.

I certainly didn't want to at the moment but he was the only person that would know what to do. And the only person I knew who had the facilities to take the puppies anyway. If they were left here overnight, it would be unlikely they would survive, they were so tiny.

I stroked Alfie's head again and again and pulled him close for a hug,

'What a good boy you are, Alfie,' I told him as, shaking now with the cold, my teeth chattering, I scrolled through my phone, the contact Puppy Love so easy to find, and pressed a button to make the call.

13

The phone rang and rang and rang . . . *Come on Jack, where are you?*

Maybe he was on his own and busy dealing with customers but surely Kayleigh would be there?

What should I do? I was so cold now and no way could I run home, get warm clothing and all the paraphernalia I would need for the puppies, and leave them here alone. It would take far too long. And anyway, if I did leave them here, someone might come and spirit them away and I so wanted to take them to Puppy Love, to Jack. Jack would definitely want to see them and they were so beautiful that they'd be snapped up in no time . . . if only I could get them there.

These thoughts went racing through my mind as I waited, but then at last, someone picked up. 'Good afternoon Puppy Love Dog & Cat Sanctuary, how can I help?'

A female voice! With a terrifying jolt I thought it was Paula but, with recognition slowly dawning, I said, 'Becky?'

'Mum?'

Desperately wanting to know what she was doing there again but keeping my curiosity at bay for now, I said, 'Look Becky, this is an emergency, OK? Is Jack there?'

'Yes, but he's busy with customers. We all are, it's crazy today.'

'OK, I'm on a run with Alfie and — '

'Oh — that's cool.'

'No — listen Becky, please, Alfie has found seven abandoned puppies in a bush right up on the tops near the cairn. I think they're beagles but I'm not sure. There's no box or blanket, no food or drink, please ask Jack to come straight away. I'm worried about them surviving ... OK?' The wind had picked up now and pulled roughly at my hair, blowing it in front of my eyes so I could barely see and the signal for the phone was getting weaker and weaker.

'Oh my God, OK . . . I'll tell him like . . . now!'

'Yes, oh and Becky, ask him if he'll bring me a blanket, or a fleece top, or anything, I'm freezing now after running all the way up here and I'm cooling down too fast. And a box or a carrier for the puppies . . . and blankets . . . '

'OK.'

'You know where the cairn is, don't you?'

'Yes, but I'll stay here with Kayleigh. Tom knows where it is, he'll come to you with Jack.'

I waited then, rubbing my hands together, blowing on them to keep them warm, and running on the spot, but I couldn't stop shivering and shaking, and my teeth chattered like malicious gossips. I felt as if my whole skeleton was quivering, the bones knocking together.

What was that song we used to sing at school?

Dem bones, dem bones, dem dry bones, the toe bone's connected to the foot bone, the foot bone's connected to the ankle bone, the ankle bone's connected to the leg bone, now shake dem skeleton bones!

Yes, that was it. I smiled to myself as memories flooded back. Wrapping my arms tightly around my body, the bone song still going round and round in my head, I noticed with total shock that, while I'd been pacing up and down trying to keep warm, Alfie had crawled into the little den inside the bushes and laid himself down among the puppies, keeping them warm like a big fluffy electric blanket. I hunkered down and peered in to get a better look.

'What a clever boy you are, Alfie,' I whispered. He opened one eye and looked at me as if to say, 'Shush hooman, we're sleeping.'

And it looked as if they really were, their tiny bodies heaving up and down as they snuffled and whimpered from their cosy places against Alfie's toasty fur.

The cold was unbearable now so, without any hesitation whatsoever, I crawled in too, feeling the damp earth and leaves against my skin and the pungent smell of the woods in my nostrils. I spooned with Alfie and the puppies like Mowgli in *The Jungle Book* until the shivering and shaking eased and then gradually stopped.

The leg bone's connected to the knee bone, the knee bone's connected to the thigh bone, the thigh bone's connected to the hip bone, now shake dem skeleton bones!

★ ★ ★

'Laurel, Laurel, what on earth are you singing? Laurel . . .'

I felt myself being shaken.

'No, no, don't shake me, I'm not the salt . . . now shake dem skeleton bones!'

'Hey, come on, Laurel, wake up . . .'

Who was this? This voice was panicky and afraid.

'Mrs Masters? I mean Laurel . . . it's Tom, please wake up . . .'

'Woof . . . woof, woof, woof . . .'

'Look Alfie's here . . . Alfie wants you to wake up . . .'

Then fingers tapped my face, tiny little taps, and then harsh breathing and something rough and wet against my cheek . . . tiny little woofs, woofs, woofs, and then slowly, very slowly, my eyes began to open . . . as if for all this time they'd been stuck. How? Superglue? Blu-Tack?

'She's opening her eyes . . . '

A face hung above me, blurry and indistinct, slowly bit by bit clearing like a mist burning away under the rays of a hot sun to reveal a beautiful day.

I can see clearly now the rain has gone . . .

His eyes were blue, bright blue, framed by long black lashes, his mouth was a strawberry waiting to be kissed, his cheekbones so chiselled they cut like a knife.

'Jack?'

'Laurel! Thank God, you're awake, stay that way, come on . . . put this on,' He was all business now as he pulled me towards him and helped me put on a fleece. It felt warm and cosy against my chilly skin. I sat up, my head swimming and my teeth chattering again.

'Here — drink this.'

I breathed in the smell of Bovril as I gulped the hot meaty liquid gratefully. Alfie came to me and licked my cheek and I pressed him close, tears that just wouldn't stop falling, soaking into his fur. 'There, there, don't cry,' soothed Jack and to my surprise kissed the top of my head making a delicious shiver run all the way down my spine.

Doing my best to ignore it, I sniffed, 'Where are the puppies?'

'In here,' replied Tom, lifting up a carrying box by the handle so that I could see them inside crawling and jostling blindly against each other like tiny pieces of moving fur.

Alfie went to the carrier and pressed his nose against it and then came back to me, tongue lolling in a smile.

'Come on,' said Jack, taking hold of my arm, 'It's only a short walk to the van.'

The smile he gave me made me feel warm inside and, like a miracle, I felt so much better than I had earlier. Or was it just the heat of the Bovril snaking through my veins and the softness of the fleece against my skin?

Tom put the carrier containing the puppies into the back of the van with Alfie, who bounded in energetically. I got into the front with Tom and Jack and off we went to the sanctuary, Jack driving quickly and easily along the windy roads, his hands relaxed on the wheel, and the beautiful Cobby countryside a green and brown blur rushing along beside us.

★ ★ ★

What a day, I thought as I sat in the sitting room later that evening, Alfie, twitching and dreaming in his sleep, laid out long in front of the fire. Oh, to see his dreams! By the movement of his legs I'd guess that he's on a good long run, the seven tiny puppies bounding along beside him.

We'd named them for the Seven Dwarves — Bashful, Doc, Dopey, Grumpy, Happy, Sleepy and Sneezy. It's just as well they were all male, wasn't it? Not one female in sight. Even so, I had a feeling that some of those names would be changed when they were eventually adopted.

There was a lot of oohing and aahing over the puppies when we brought them in with Becky and Kayleigh hanging over them like mother hens.

'I'll take them to the vet next week,' Jack told us all. 'They'll need a good checking over along with any injections he'll advise them to have. After that, we can let people look at them with a view to adoption.'

Turning to Alfie, he said solemnly, 'Alfie, you truly are a wonder dog. Very good work!' and presented him with what looked like a year's supply of dog food and treats.

However while he was very interested in his gifts, Alfie seemed to prefer to stay close to the puppies in their new home, a blanket-lined basket on the floor close to the office heater. Becky and Kayleigh tied a massive red bow around his neck, which looked magnificent against the deep black of his fur.

The sound of Robbie and Ash laughing echoed down the stairs from Robbie's bedroom. I was intrigued as to what computer game was causing such hilarity. Ash was on a sleepover here for a change, and Becky and Tom had gone to the hospital to see Danny.

Danny was facing at least another six weeks in hospital while waiting for his pelvis to heal. You can cope with a broken leg at home, but a pelvis? No not so well! I'd bet anybody a tenner that he regretted ever even looking at Tom's bike on that fateful evening, let alone stealing it!

I sipped at a glass of wine, which ran through my veins like fire. I breathed in deeply, trying to relax, the events of the day running through my mind.

Jack had wanted to take me out for a drink tonight but I'd refused again.

'No, Jack,' I told him. 'We said a month remember? And anyway, I'm not exactly in the mood this evening. It's been quite a day, you know.'

He looked disappointed but said, 'OK, Laurel. Soon, then?'

And when I just nodded, my face a mask, he said, 'If it's Paula you're worried about, she won't bother us again. I sent her packing on Thursday night. I was so embarrassed, Laurel. Did Paul and Stephen tell you what she was like?'

'Yes,' I said, 'I think Stephen said something like, 'What a piece of work she is!"

Jack laughed heartily, showing all his lovely white teeth. Mr Hollywood indeed!

'He's not wrong there. To tell you the truth, Laurel, I think she has serious issues and should see a doctor perhaps, or a counsellor. She acts very erratically — did Paul and Stephen tell you that she tried to attack me with a glass? I had a lucky escape thanks to them.'

'I know,' I said, 'Yes, I do think Paula has problems. I thought that before I met her, when I first met you and you told me the Donny Osmond débacle. That's just not normal behaviour for a grown woman. I have a really bad feeling that we haven't seen the last of her, Jack.'

'No — trust me,' he said. 'I told her to go and not to come to the sanctuary again. She knows that I know everything; I know all her lies, that the baby isn't mine and that she's taken over a thousand pounds of my money from the safe. I said that if she showed her face again, I'd have to report her to the police.'

'Well, I'm not sure. I have a funny feeling in my water,' I told him. 'Keep your eyes peeled at all times, Jack. It wouldn't surprise me if she turned up here again.

'Did she threaten you or anything like that after you told her that you knew she'd been lying about everything?'

'Oh yeah — you know, like *I'll get even with you*, that sort of thing . . . just silly empty threats.' He shrugged.

'That sounds ominous to me, and not empty threats at all. Make sure you're never alone here. Paula is dangerous.'

'Hmm.' He gave a little chuckle. 'You and your hunches . . . and now a feeling in your water?'

Absentmindedly he fiddled with the stubble on his chin, the action making my heart heat rev up by several notches. Why did he do that in front of me? Didn't he realise how sexy it looked? And with that as well as the slice of tanned chest that I could see at the neck of his shirt, I was beginning to feel far too hot.

'Talking of not being alone here, Tom wants to come in more often, to train alongside me. He's mentioned that he wants to become a vet. He's been asking my advice.'

'Wow, that's wonderful! He's such a nice boy and so good for Becky. The two of them, and Robbie, are going to meet Will's girlfriend Liz next weekend. Becky wouldn't have done that before she started seeing Tom. She was so bitter against her dad and yet now I feel that she's changing, and any bad feeling is disappearing.'

'She's growing up, beginning to understand the situation between you and Will. Yes, Tom's a very intelligent young man.' He scratched his chin and said thoughtfully, 'If only I could afford to pay him ... just a small wage while he's training ... then he wouldn't have to work in Yarrows.'

'Yes, that would be really good ... he does a lot of hours there, but, as you say, you can't afford it — can you?'

'I'm not sure. Is there some initiative that pays employers for training a young person? Like an apprenticeship? Well, that's what it was called when I was young.'

'I think there's something called a Go-For-It Scheme, it's something to do with the Regular Payment Project. Becky will know about it I'm sure, I'll ask her. Or you can.'

'Yes, I will, that's certainly something to think about. Thank you, Laurel.'

How caring he is about young people, I thought. He was genuinely interested in helping Tom, and I was so glad that he seemed at ease with Becky and Robbie too.

He stared at me for a moment or two and then, without warning, came closer and put his arms around me, pulling me into an embrace. The musky odour of his aftershave was all around and I breathed it in like an aphrodisiac as my face was pressed into him, against that little bit of hairy chest and his smooth, clean neck.

I felt the muscles in his broad shoulders as his arms snaked around my waist. I wanted to melt into him, raise my face and let my lips meet his luscious strawberry ones, but I couldn't . . . not yet.

I pulled away with all my strength and said, 'No, Jack, please . . . I'm not ready for that.'

The yearning look on his face said it all.

'Oh Laurel, please let me put it right . . . I don't want things between us to be over before they've even begun.'

'I don't know, Jack,' I said shaking my head. 'I really don't know at the moment. I need to think.'

Tiny little whines brought me out of my thoughts and I saw Alfie standing in front of me, fully awake now and desperate to go outside by the look of him.

If a dog could be cross-legged then right now he definitely would be, just like one of those weird toilet door signs of a man or a woman cross legged but a dog instead. The thought made me smile.

'Come on then, boy,' I said, as I got up wearily from the chair, rolling my shoulders and stretching. 'Let's go for a walk around the block.'

Jumping up and down as if on a pogo stick, tongue lolling, Alfie waited until, coat and boots on, a hat on my head and gloves on my hands, I was ready. Then we stepped outside, my shoulders hunched to my ears, into the cold night air.

★ ★ ★

Kath was in Cobby Cuts and Curls for her six-weekly trim and colour and I was telling her the tale about the puppies and, bragging of course, about Alfie the wonder dog and how clever he was.

It was busy today in the salon and noisy with the radio playing and hair dryers whining, as well as all the chit-chat between the staff and customers. The air was suffused with the odour of coconut shampoo and strawberry conditioner and all the other wonderful lotions and potions that we put on our customers' hair to make it look and smell good.

'Oh, how wonderful that you and Alfie saved the puppies. That was quite a find,' Kath said, 'Are they ready for adoption yet? What breed are they?'

'They're beagles,' I told her, as I carefully trimmed her hair, keeping it shoulder length as she liked it. 'Jack is having them checked over at the vet this week, but I can let you know when they're ready if you want me to.'

'Oh yes, please do, Laurel. My dog, Honey, is getting on a bit. I'm sure a puppy would give her a new lease of life. Have they been named yet?'

With a laugh I told her the names but said that of course they could be changed, but straight away, she said, 'I'd like the one called Happy!'

'Then Happy will be yours,' I said with a flourish. 'Although really you should see them before choosing. They all have such different personalities and Happy may not be the puppy for you . . . just saying.' I looked at her in the mirror, making sure that her fringe looked nice and straight above her eyebrows.

She nodded and said she understood exactly what I meant and to let her know when she could come to the sanctuary to look at them. We then went on to talk about my and Maggie's boggy gardens.

I could barely hear her over the noise of the hairdryer but the gist of it was that the subject was going on the full town council agenda again in another couple of weeks. A representative from the Environment Agency had agreed to come, as had a member of the Skelmanthorpe District Planning Office but, so far, there'd been no response from the builders.

'But that's typical,' Kath told me as I held a mirror so she had a good view of the back of her new hairdo, 'They're slippery as eels . . . really they are, Laurel.'

She nodded at the reflection and said,

'That's lovely, thank you.'

As she was paying, she whispered discreetly, 'I do hope things are going OK with you and Jack now?'

I shrugged and said, 'I'm not sure, Kath . . . he's on a month's trial!'

'Really?' she asked, raising her eyebrows, 'Well, you've got him where you want him then?'

'I'm not sure,' I said with a grin.

And leaning in closer to me she whispered, 'He really is an extraordinarily handsome man, Laurel.'

She gave me a wink as she went out of the door and I watched her as she stood outside for a few minutes, carefully putting on a hat over her sleek hair and pulling on a pair of leather gloves. I wondered as I always did whether she still missed her husband, Johnny Emmerson, now that she was married to the very delectable Paul Timpson. According to rumour, Kath had been very much in love with Johnny and had taken a long time to recover from such a devastating shock as his early death.

I could identify with her in a way as it was traumatic enough getting over the divorce of a husband let alone a bereavement. I was fine with it now, though, and glad that Will had found happiness with someone else.

Thinking of Will made me think of Becky and what she'd said after their meeting with his girlfriend, Liz Fletcher.

'She's really nice, Mum, but expect a call from her at the salon asking for an appointment. I recommended you.'

'Oh yes . . . what's her hair like?'

I tried to remember the woman I'd seen with Will all those weeks ago but could only remember her long hair being dark and glossy and definitely not in need of a makeover.

'A frizzy mess,' Becky told me, eyes wide. 'Apparently she went to a new hairdresser in Skelly and they absolutely butchered her hair.'

'Butchered it?'

'Yeah — those are her words, not mine.'

I told her I'd be pleased to sort out Liz's

hair and would make her an appointment when she called. I then changed the subject and asked whether Jack had made any mention of the Go-For-It Scheme?

She said that he had and that both she and Tom had to go to the job centre to fill in all the relevant forms for the Regular Payment Project before they could be on the scheme.

'You as well? You don't want to be a vet too do you, Becky?'

'No,' she said but I'm interested in doing the same sort of scheme in Skelly, in the hospital. I think I'd like to be a nurse. What do you think, Mum?'

'I think that's a great idea,' I told her. 'You certainly looked after me the other day — a suitably bossy nurse, I would say.'

She giggled and once again I thanked God that Becky had met Tom. She'd been a changed girl ever since. Who would have thought that her having a boyfriend would have made so much difference? Not me . . . that's for sure!

And to think I'd been so worried about

the effect his wild brother Danny's activities might have on him. Well, it just goes to show that brothers definitely don't follow in each other's footsteps, and I needn't have worried at all.

14

'The trial month is up today,' announced Jack as I took a seat at my desk, in the office building at the sanctuary, a full mug in one hand and a biscuit in the other. 'So I propose that you join me tonight in the Star pub for a drink or two, at which point I would like to know my score.'

'Your score?' I asked him, as I took a deep draught of coffee and took a bite out of the biscuit.

'Yes, you said you would give me marks out of ten after the trial period. I'm very much hoping that you'll award me the full quota.'

He paced up and down, his hands behind his back, and then stopped suddenly and peered from the window like a lord inspecting his land.

'Oh really,' I said lightly. 'And why, good Sir, do you think that I should award you top marks? What have you done to deserve such an honour?'

'I'll tell you later . . . tonight in the pub.'

He turned around with a grin. His teeth looked very white and his eyes very blue.

'Your friends, Kath and Maggie, are here. Come to look at the puppies, I suppose.'

I joined him at the window. The sun was trying to come out from behind clouds that were piled like pillows in a pewter-grey sky. Trees shook in the breeze.

'Oh yes — brilliant! I wonder if Maggie wants a puppy too.'

I crunched over to where my friends stood at the puppy cages, peering in alongside Kayleigh and Tom. Tom was working his notice at Yarrows and almost ready to take up his place alongside Jack as part of the Go-For-It Scheme. He and Kayleigh both went off to do other jobs so that I could deal with Maggie and Kath.

'Hi,' I said. 'So good to see you two.'

'Hi Laurel . . . I couldn't wait any

longer,' said Kath. 'Which one's Happy?'

'There,' I said pointing. 'The one with the white coat and one brown ear.'

There were only three pups left now and they were tumbling around together, biting and growling as if they were out in the wild. The air felt fresh and clean. A sharp wind blew our hair and lifted Kath's skirt so she had to grab the hem and pull it down.

Maggie gave me a friendly nod. 'Hello, Laurel.'

'Do you want one too, Maggie?'

'Ooh, no,' she replied, 'I've got my old cat, Arthur, and he wouldn't be at all pleased if I brought a puppy home. I just came along with Kath for some moral support.'

I had to grin at the thought of Maggie's old cat, Arthur, a mangy ginger tom. I often saw him stalking our garden for birds or mice until Alfie chased him away.

'Oh yes,' said Kath, her eyes wide. 'That's the one I want, definitely — Happy. There aren't many left now, are there?'

'No — if you take Happy, there'll only be Doc and Sneezy left.'

A couple of other people broke away from the group milling around the cats' cages, and wandered over to look at the puppies.

Carefully I opened the door to the cage and managed to get the squirming puppy out. I held him out to Kath and, carefully, she took him into her arms bringing him close to her face so she could kiss the very top of his head.

'Oh, my grandchildren, Layla and Joe, will love him. They're already in love with Honey, but he is so cute.'

'Actually Laurel, Kath and I have something to ask you — '

I turned to them questioningly just as Jack came out of the office building and sauntered towards us. Well, sauntered is the wrong word, more like prowled over to us like a sleek panther.

A sleek, sexy panther, I thought, wondering what marks out of ten I would be giving him that evening in the pub. Because I knew, didn't I, that I would be going out with him that night. I'd done a lot of thinking over the past month and I'd made my decision. All I had to do now was tell Jack what it was. The wind had tousled his hair making him look even more rugged and appealing.

'Hello, ladies,' he said casually. 'Did you get the puppy you wanted, Kath?'

They both nodded, flustered, as women always seemed to be around Jack, and Kath said, 'Oh yes, I'm taking Happy.'

'Happy what?' said Jack with a grin. 'Pills?' That caused all-round general laughter before I said to the two of them, 'So what did you want to ask me?'

Kath said, 'Well, I was wondering, Laurel — have you ever considered becoming a councillor?'

'A councillor? Well, no, I haven't. Not at all.'

'You seemed to enjoy being in the council chamber when we made our speech,' said Maggie. 'And, well . . . '

'Councillor Melrose is going to run for District,' said Kath 'If he gets on . . . well, there'll be a vacancy.'

'Oh . . . is that the councillor who does impersonations of Eric Morecambe?'

'Yes, that's him . . . he's quite mad, you know!' I don't know why but I glanced at Jack, who gave me a nod of his head and a raise of the eyebrows.

'I've got to admit,' he said. 'I can just see you as a Councillor, Laurel. Yes, Councillor Masters, you could organise a fun run or some sort of sporting event.'

'We already do a fun run,' said Kath, 'organised by Maggie as part of the events and leisure committee, but we never say no to extra help.'

With the promise that I would think about it, we went to the office and dealt with the usual paperwork for the adoption of Happy. I watched them walk to the car, Kath hugging the puppy close to her before reluctantly placing him in his carrier and Maggie taking it on her knee in the passenger seat. I saw Maggie peer inside and give the puppy a little wiggly wave as Kath drove slowly away.

I went back to the office and worked

steadily until the sun disappeared altogether behind those grey banked clouds and darkness started to fall. Kayleigh and Tom went home as Jack and I did one last check of the animals, going slowly and carefully from one pen to the other, making sure they were all locked up and comfortable for the night.

A young couple had adopted Doc and Sneezy just after Kath had taken Happy, so their pen stood bare and forlorn now that all the puppies were gone.

'Well,' I said, 'they've all gone to their fur-ever homes, Jack.'

In a strange way, everything seemed a bit of an anticlimax now that the puppies weren't there. I'd so enjoyed seeing them rough and tumble together and watch how their different personalities came to the fore as they grew up.

I must have sounded sad and wistful because Jack said encouragingly, 'You should be glad, Laurel. They wouldn't be going to their fur-ever homes if it wasn't for you and Alfie. You saved their lives, that's for sure.'

There was a short silence as we walked back to the office, content that the animals were safe for the night. I checked my watch and saw that it was a lot later than I had thought. I was usually on my way home by now and, if we were meeting tonight, I would need to get home in order to make myself look suitably alluring for The Star pub (or for Jack?). It was just as well that Becky was walking Alfie today.

Just as I was wondering whether or not our date was still on, Jack said, 'So will I see you tonight?'

I reached for my coat and began to put it on, buttoning it slowly and carefully as I peeked beneath my lashes at the expression on his face. Was that hopefulness that I saw there in those sexy blue eyes?

'Umm . . . OK, yes that will be great, Jack. About eight o'clock in The Star?'

He gave me his megawatt Hollywood smile as he picked up his jacket, the very attractive muscles in his shoulders rippling as he shrugged it on.

'Yes, eight o'clock in The Star, I can't wait.' He started singing in quite a rich melodic voice — maybe he really was Mr Hollywood. '*Tonight, tonight, won't be just any night . . .* '

'Stop it, Jack!' I said, laughing and nudging him in the ribs.

'*Tonight there will be no morning star . . .* '

Still laughing, we locked the office door and crunched our way over to my car and the Puppy Love van.

'You have a good voice,' I told him.

'In that case I will serenade you some more.' He raised his arms and sang strong and proud,

'*Tonight, tonight, I'll see my love tonight . . .* '

Giggling, I said, 'Jack!'

With a smile, he coiled his arm around my waist as we walked. Drawing me close to him, he kissed the top of my head, his lips soft as the touch of a feather. Gently he pulled me around until our bodies met, slotting together as if we were truly meant to be.

I gazed up at him, at his eyes that

glowed like sapphires in the gloom and his mouth red and ripe that hovered unbearably for a heartbeat and then came closer and closer to mine.

With a jolt I pulled away, and whispered, 'Jack — I heard something.'

I was absolutely sure that I'd seen something too, right at the very edge of my vision. A flash of white, a blur, I don't know what, but I knew that something or somebody was there.

My first thought was Paula. I could be wrong, but I had a hunch she'd come back. Overhead the sky was a suffocating black, stars spread out over its surface twinkling gaily as precious stones and the air was cold. So very cold, since I'd pulled away from the warmth of Jack's body.

His head snapped up and, eyes narrowed, he stared into the blackness, all his senses it seemed heightened like a hunter alert for the kill. He reminded me of Alfie when he stalked Maggie's old cat, Arthur.

Clutching hands we edged away from our cars and into the deep darkness of the surrounding bushes, avoiding the security lights that we knew would come on if they spotted us.

'What do you think?' Jack asked softly, 'Have you a feeling in your water?'

'Stop it, Jack.' I nudged him with my elbow. 'This is serious! There's somebody here!'

No sooner had I said those words than I heard a whispered voice.

'Be careful, they might still be here.'

This voice had an accent, something foreign. Italian maybe? Was it George, the person Paula had been talking to on the phone? The person who knew all about her little schemes and, in fact, encouraged them?

'No, everything's locked up for the night. So it's now or never . . .'

The moon — a tiny sliver, a waning moon — peeked out from the banked up clouds that had kept the sun from shining earlier, throwing a narrow beam of light onto the animals' cages. I could hear them sniffing and snuffling, the cats mewing and the dogs' incessant soft barking, the presence of strangers making them anxious and afraid.

'It's Paula,' said Jack quietly. 'I've got to say the feelings in your water should never be ignored.'

'Don't joke . . . please.' I shook my head irritably, feeling very scared now, coiled tight as a spring.

Paula was unstable, making me wonder what she was going to do. *It's now or never* — what did that mean? I had an awful feeling it was something bad, and I feared for the animals.

The glaring light of the moon must have revealed our cars for the accented voice said softly, 'We better go, Paula, their cars are here. We should have noticed them before. Come on . . . come on . . .'

How amateurish they are, I thought as they started to creep away, Paula lumbering awkwardly next to a skinny man who I assumed was George. Jack seemed to relax a little, his hand in mine lessening its grip, when suddenly Paula changed tack and ran forward, towards the animal's cages, the red can she was holding swinging in her hand, spilling what smelled like petrol all over the ground.

Before I could react, Jack sprang up and ran to her, the muscles in his neck standing out like ropes as the word 'Nooooooooooo!' reverberated throughout the still clear air.

★　★　★

'Cheers, Laurel,' said Jack, raising his glass high.

'Cheers,' I echoed, raising my glass too. I was so glad that I was here at last in the Star pub, sitting next to the wood-burning stove, my cold hands spread out towards the roaring red and gold flames and a glass of very good red wine on the table beside me.

Jack, for all his Hollywood good looks, appeared exhausted now which was just as I felt after the trauma that we'd endured tonight. We hadn't even bothered to go home to get changed, which said a lot about both our states of mind. I'm sure that if I'd been in a better mood, I would have felt quite dowdy in my office clothes compared to the trendy outfits that most of the young people in here seemed to be wearing.

Jack took a deep draught from his pint, the froth coating his lips that he licked off with a pointed tongue making my heart rev up a beat or two.

'I'm sorry that you've got caught up in all this, Laurel, I really am. I didn't realise how evil Paula could be. I mean, throwing petrol at defenceless animals is the lowest of the low.'

'Thank God we were there and you stopped her,' I said, taking a comforting sip of wine which travelled straight through my veins like a shot of adrenaline. 'You ran at her faster than a greyhound at a race track! I can see you joining me and Alfie in a run to Cobby Cairn soon!'

We both laughed uproariously and several old men sitting in the corner playing dominoes stopped and stared.

'Yes . . . don't laugh, Laurel, but I might just do that one day. You never know. I could quite see myself as a run-ner.'

Yes — I thought I could too, especially wearing the running gear of little shorts and a vest top. Before I got too excited at the images of Jack I could see in my mind's eye and to change the subject back to Paula, I said, 'Do you think she really would have lit that match after she threw the petrol?'

'Yes, I do,' replied Jack staunchly.

'So you understand why I called the police?'

'Yes, of course, attempting to set a fire is just as dangerous as setting it. And if she hadn't done it then, she would have come back and tried again.'

'Yes,' I answered as I gazed into the flames — flames that I realised were scary and dangerous if used in the wrong way. 'She really was determined to get even with you Jack . . .'

'Yes — through the animals, the place where she knew it would hurt me the most! And I've got to say her face was a picture when the police arrived. She didn't expect that.'

I shook my head in disbelief.

'Well, what did she expect then? If you break the law, you have to pay for it, don't you?'

Jack nodded, 'Yes — you certainly do.'

'Goodness knows where that George man came into it. What do you think?'

'I've no idea. He looked a bit of a misfit to me, not Paula's usual type at all.'

'No, she seems to go for the Hollywood heart-throb type, doesn't she?' I said, giving him a bit of a look.

Jack blushed, crimson suffusing his handsome face, and said, 'Really, Laurel, looking back I don't think she wanted me for me, let alone my looks, but what she could get from me. The business, money, that's all that was on her mind.'

A few of the old men stood up and went off to the bar, squeezing past groups of people talking loudly together, empty glasses clutched in their hands. Beautiful heart-rending music echoed from the jukebox — *I'm saving all my love for you.*

'Aah, Whitney Houston,' said Jack

appreciatively. 'My favourite singer.'

I agreed. 'Yes, and she was so beautiful, too.'

'Talking about beauty,' he said, leaning forward to take my hand, 'and you truly have that . . . '

'Oh, Jack . . . '

'Will you go out with me, Laurel?'

'I feel like a teenager,' I said shyly.

'Please . . . be mine.' He increased the pressure of his fingers on my hand and my stomach clenched in a most pleasing way. 'If I had one of those Love Heart sweets with such a declaration printed on it, I would give it to you . . . and only you.'

I giggled like a girl and trembled at the expression in his eyes but, trying to put on a straight face, I said sternly, 'I can't possibly say yes. Not until I've given you your trial marks out of ten.'

'Do I need another drink?' He nodded towards his almost empty pint.

'Yes,' I told him. 'I really think you do!'

'Bad news, then?'

'Hmm, maybe . . . maybe not. If you

buy me another drink, I will reveal all.'

Slowly he stood up and, collecting our glasses, began to walk to the bar, his stride long and easy and a pleasure to watch. There was a whirr and a click from the jukebox, a little bit of background static and then, *She's a perfect ten, but she wears a twelve . . .*

He stopped mid-stride and turning his head, grinning, said, 'You set that up!'

'No,' I said, shaking my head. 'No, I didn't.'

All the little old men turned around to stare as, with just a touch of hysteria, I laughed and laughed until tears, salty and warm, ran down my cheeks.

15

Standing once again at the top of Cobby Cairn, heart thumping like a wild thing, my breath short and shallow and my fingers on the cool roughness of the trig stone, I surveyed my surroundings from afar like a queen from the lofty pedestal of her throne.

Alfie panted beside me and then darted away to sniff the bushes hoping, I think, to discover some more cute squirming puppies in their cool leafy depths which, because of spring, are covered in a new growth of soft green buds.

Watching Alfie I realise that it was right here in these very bushes that Alfie and I lay down with the puppies, all of us trying to keep each other warm. I think I must have had runner's 'shivers' that day from cooling down too quickly. Jack told me later that I was singing when he arrived to help, a song from school that I hadn't even thought of for years, let alone sung — '*dem bones, dem bones, dem dry bones, now shake dem skeleton bones.*' Now why that song? Hmm . . . a touch delirious,perhaps?

Cobby was laid out in front of me in all its glory. I took it all in, reveling in its beauty, leafy trees swaying in the breeze and the canal rich with wildlife meandering slowly along. There was a patchwork quilt of fields, emerald and yellow, and the hedgerows were black and crimson with fruit, amidst the roads and pavements and the red roofs of houses. Dry stone walls were grey against the greenery and I saw clusters of shops and the black Tarmac of playgrounds, children, tiny as ants, playing on the swings and the slides. Cars glinted in the sunshine as they raced on the bypass or drove the winding roads like a fairground ride.

I called to Alfie and he ran towards me, ears flapping and tongue hanging long, and we began the descent back into Cobby. My mind was racing with all the things that had happened throughout the past few months, particularly with the evil Paula Lee and her attempt to burn down the sanctuary.

That night played out in my mind again and again, and I relived the panic I felt as she ran towards the animals' cages, the red can swinging from her hand and the smell of petrol, greasy and warm, hanging in the air, making me gag and choke.

I'd hunkered down in the bushes out of the way, not wanting her to see me. Quietly I made my 999 call as Paula railed at Jack for the way he'd treated her, saying that she would take him to court, and that the Puppy Love sanctuary should be sold and half of the proceeds go to her because the business had been all her idea and all her efforts had gone into it.

She warned him against 'that Laurel' because I was a single parent and only after a meal ticket and why couldn't he see that? After a while, sick to the back teeth of listening to her monologue, I covered my ears with my hands. Even Jack told me later in the pub that he'd wished he'd had something to gag her with. 'Especially when she started to say nasty things about you, Laurel.'

The elusive George, or Giorgio as I liked to think of him, disappeared, sidled away into the darkness never to be seen again, but Jack had managed to get a firm hold of Paula with his quick actions and she was taken away for questioning, along with the petrol can as incriminating evidence, by the police, who arrived quickly, blue light flashing.

'Do you know,' I heard one of the officers say as Paula got into the car, 'you could get a hefty prison sentence just for attempted arson.'

* * *

We were almost home now, running along the tow path, dodging around all the people out for an early morning walk with their dogs, or cyclists tinkling their bells. There were also other runners, some with faithful pets like Alfie bounding along beside them. The water was thick with ducks and geese that hissed and spat. A family of swans sailed by, their skinny legs working rapidly beneath the water, the cygnets grey and fluffy as chicks.

My thoughts turned to Becky and Tom and the accident. What trauma she had suffered when she thought it was Tom lying on the road, badly injured amongst the wreckage of his bike, and what a feeling of relief when she found out that it wasn't him at all.

Danny was fully recovered now and, according to Tom, a changed man.

'I've never seen anybody so sorry,' said Tom, shaking his head. 'He can't do enough to make it up to me for stealing and writing off my bike, and he's been coming to the sanctuary to help out, so Jack has got himself another willing volunteer. Oh, and he's definitely keeping on the right side of the law now.'

'Hey, don't get too many people interested in the sanctuary,' I remembered saying to him with a smile. 'I don't want anyone taking my job!'

Tom had a new bike now and according to Robbie, 'It's green and shiny and really ace . . . ' And also he knows the registration number, 'But it's not unusual like the one on his old bike. Just an ordinary run of the mill registration plate,' he said, disappointment evident on his face.

Becky was pleased that Tom had a new bike but still adamant that she'd never ride pillion, the accident itself being enough to put her off forever.

'Huh,' I remembered her saying. 'I'd rather wear my trainee nurse's uniform than a crash helmet!' And I'm keeping my fingers crossed that she'll always think that way.

We were running through Cobby village now, past Bloomers, the usual long queue straggling out of the door, now Cobby Cuts and Curls where the girls gave me strange looks as I ran by and I heard someone say, 'Hey, Laurel, don't you think you should be at home by now?'

I flew as if I have wings on my heels past Bedrock & Rose, the little balcony bare now of those lovely cascading plants that used to brighten up the street. It was empty at the moment as Will had moved with Liz Fletcher to a very upmarket semi-detached house in Hampthwaite. I thought Jack was considering taking over Will's flat but we weren't so sure now. Circumstances had changed — oh yes, our situation was very different from what it was just a few months ago.

I was almost back home and as I turned the corner into my own road, the notorious White Church Lane, I saw Kath and Paul Timpson hurrying from Maggie's house. They did a double take when they saw me, Paul raising his hands palms up, and Kath frowning, pointing forcefully at her watch with a finger.

'Really, Laurel . . . you should have been back ages ago.'

What's all that about? I thought as I gave them a little wiggly wave of the fingers and carried on running because I was so nearly there and I couldn't stop now. Alfie was in the lead, a black blur as we turned into our garden and that's when I stopped and stood on the path, hands on my thighs, slightly bent over and trying to catch my breath.

Maggie's old cat Arthur sauntered past Alfie who lunged at him with a way-ward paw but, slippery as an eel, Arthur disappeared over the fence, orange eyes flashing and claws outspread.

Alfie, dumbstruck it seemed at the quickness of old Arthur, sat back on his haunches and gazed at me, a soulful look in his deep brown eyes as he watched me stretch.

'You should be doing this too, Alfie,' I tell him, 'It's what you're supposed to do after a run.'

Maggie's bedroom window suddenly opened and she leaned out. For some strange reason she was still wearing a bright blue dressing gown and what looked like a nightgown underneath, but I noticed that her face was made up with eyeshadow and a bright red lipstick and her hair billowed around her head in a mass of beautiful dark curls.

'Laurel, really,' she said. 'Shouldn't you be inside by now?' Energetically she tapped her watch with a finger, and before I could say anything, before I could ask what on earth she was on about, she shook her head and pulled the window closed with a thud.

Indoors everything was quiet, except for the whoosh of the shower from the bathroom and the faint thump of music from Becky's room — or was it Robbie's? I went into the kitchen and put the kettle on. It purred into life like Maggie's old cat, Arthur, as I put coffee and sugar into a mug. Alfie begged for treats and I gave him some shaped like little brown bones, throwing each one up in the air so he could jump up and catch them in his mouth like a ball.

Wandering into the sitting room, I settled into an easy chair, Alfie at my feet, his head on his paws, ready for sleep. Our run had worn him out. I sipped coffee from my mug. My heart rate had slowed now and my body felt tingly and alive, and a feeling of happiness engulfed me. Endorphins were attacking my brain . . . I must be on a runner's high. Alfie dreamed at my feet, skinny legs cycling as if he were riding a bike.

I gazed out of the window at the garden. The daffodils were in bloom, and bright yellow clumps gleamed everywhere like patches of gold. In the borders, around the apple tree, on the grass — grass that is boggy no more thanks to what is called a Catch Basin, a clever little thing that had drained all the water away from the grass with the help of pipes that zig-zagged beneath the surface. It was very kindly installed for me (and for Maggie of course) by Jack with a little help from his friends Paul Timpson and Stephen Gates. We had had no joy at all from the builders who completely ignored their invitation to the full town council meeting.

Bringing me out of my reverie I heard Becky's voice and looked up to see her standing in front of me, hands on hips that cannot be seen as she's encased from head to toe in a fluffy white towel and another smaller one wrapped turban style around her head. Robbie hovered uncertainly at her elbow.

'For God's sake, Mum,' she said, her face bright red from the shower. 'Where have you been? Don't you think you should at least attempt to get ready?'

'Yeah, Mum, I'm almost there,' piped up Robbie, 'Look!' He stood with his arms outstretched, looking smart already in his new long black trousers and a bright white shirt.

'Oh,' I replied, glancing at my watch, 'I've got plenty of time yet. I don't know what everyone's getting so uptight about.'

Was it my imagination or was Becky getting bossier than ever? *I'm not bossy, I'm just helpful* would no doubt be her mantra now!

'Really?' said Becky. 'If only we could all be as laid back as you! Well, the shower's free now so maybe you'd better get in. After all, you don't want to be late for your own wedding, do you?'

16

My first wedding took place in a little church in Skelmanthorpe, or Skelly as we always call it, where I was born, and a stone's throw away from where I lived at the time with my mum and dad and brother, Rowan.

It was long before Rowan met Jane and long before Ash and Willow were even a twinkle in their daddy's eye (as the saying goes), and of course there was no Becky and there was no Robbie which I now find impossible to believe. The life I had before Becky and Robbie now seemed like some sort of vague dream — but I had Will, and I suppose I thought that I would have Will forever. Well, that's what marriage is all about, isn't it?

It took me a long time to realise that some things just aren't meant to last forever, that there's something or someone else waiting out there, something or someone that is meant to be.

What's that saying? *Every wrong turn takes you to the right place.* What I thought at first was a wrong turn — when Will and I went our separate ways — took me to the right place. To Jack. And that was why I now believed that Jack and I were meant to be.

The stars were aligned that day when I picked Puppy Love Dog And Cat Sanctuary from all the other places that came up on my online search. The day when I took Becky and Robbie to look for a dog, the very day that we found Alfie, was the very day that I found Jack.

Gazing from my bedroom window, such crazy thoughts going through my head, I saw that it was a fine spring day. A cloud-speckled blue sky arched above and a big, shiny yellow sun — just like the smiley face patch that I used to wear on my jeans so many years ago.

I recalled my wedding dress, a concoction of frills and lace and so blindingly white that it hurt my eyes. I'm surprised I didn't wear a pair of cool shades as I walked down the aisle, clinging nervously to my Dad's arm. I remembered an October sun shining softly through the huge arched windows of the church throwing spots of light, red, blue and yellow, on the stone-flagged floor.

Compared to the smart cream suit that I'm going to wear today, the dress was a frivolity, a whimsy, a dream. They called the Titanic the ship of dreams — well, my wedding dress was the dress of dreams, a young girl's fantasy. It just went to show what a hopeless romantic I was then.

After all, I was still in love with Donny Osmond, though not in the weird stalking sort of way that Paula had been. I had posters of him all over my bedroom walls, as well as glossy photos of David Cassidy and David Essex. My bed had been a mattress on the floor, and a boyfriend before Will had painted a Union Jack, taking up a whole wall, which was definitely different and looked really good.

My mum, being a bit of a hippy herself, hadn't minded my strange tastes and had encouraged me to create a collage on another wall using newspaper articles about current issues and pop stars and film stars. It made for really interesting reading. I shook my head, wondering why my wedding day was bringing back such old memories. Things that I hadn't thought about in any form for years.

I dressed slowly and carefully, gazing at myself in the mirror, wanting to look pretty for Jack. Now then . . . something old. Me?

I laugh softly and shake my head, instead fastening around my neck a silver cross that I was given by Mum and Dad for my twenty-first birthday.

Something new? I put on a pair of silver earrings bought recently from an unusual little gift shop in Cobby. Something borrowed? I'd already asked Becky — I wanted to wear something that belonged to my daughter. And last of all, something blue? A blue garter edged with lace that I pulled up one slim leg, right up to the thigh, covering it quickly with the crackly folds of my long cream skirt.

There was a little tap on the door and Becky peered in, her face artfully made up but softer now, not as harsh as before she met Tom. As my maid of honour, she wore a long sky-blue dress and a circlet of flowers like a crown on her head. 'Something borrowed, Mum?' she asked, holding out a pretty bracelet that, with thanks, I slipped on to my wrist.

'I'm sorry I was so bossy earlier,' she told me, 'But I was really scared that you wouldn't be ready on time.'

'You're not bossy,' I assured her. 'Just helpful.'

She gave a smile that lit up her face.

'Wow, yeah, you're right. I was really worried, though — I mean, who goes running on their wedding day?'

'All brides are late on their wedding day,' I assured her, as I peered once more in the mirror, checking my hair and my make-up. 'It's a tradition.'

Robbie appeared then, with Alfie at his side, a very sleek Alfie wearing a bright red bandana decorated with swirly writing. On peering closer I saw that it read,

A happy Wedding Day to Laurel and Jack.
Robbie looked super-smart in his dark trousers and jacket, set off by a sparkling white shirt and a groovy Seventies style patterned tie.

'Hey Mum, guess what?' he said.

'What, Robbie?' I asked him patiently.

'I'm glad you're going to marry Jack, he's really cool, just like Dad.'

'I'm glad you like him, Robbie.'

'And guess what, Mum?'

'What?'

'Nanny and Grandad are here! Wow — in a long black car. I can see the registration number — it's NY21 ABC . . . wow, 2021 . . . wow . . . and ABC too . . . cool!'

Becky and I exchanged smiles and I shook my head at Robbie who reminded me of Rowan who, when he was a boy, used to collect car registrations and train numbers, all neatly written down in tiny writing in hundreds and hundreds of notebooks. The fleeting thought *What happened to all those notebooks?* went through my mind.

Picking up my bouquet with its scent of spring flowers, tulips, lilac and daffodils, I peered from the window at the long black limousine that had drawn up to the kerb, showing without doubt that Mum and Dad had hired a car for the day.

I wondered yet again why Dad felt it necessary to walk me down the aisle. A woman of my age on her second marriage should perhaps have chosen the registry office to tie the knot, but it seemed so soulless, and the church in Cobby — such a beautiful old church squatting amongst its tumbledown graveyard — beckoned with an arching finger.

It was very small inside though and would literally take about twenty or thirty steps to walk the whole length of the aisle. But Dad had insisted.

'What? Your dad not walk you down the aisle on your wedding day? You must be joking. We'll come and pick you up.'

'It's my second wedding, Dad,' I reminded him.

'Who cares?' he replied shrugging

carelessly. 'It could be your fifth or even your tenth and I'd still want to walk you down the aisle.'

My tenth? I'd thought in alarm. I'd found it hard to believe that Dad would be happy with a tenth marriage. Anyhow I'd agreed to the walk down the aisle. After all, there was nothing wrong with indulging him on my wedding day.

I watched our guests filing into the church as I sat in the car wedged between Mum and Becky and Robbie. Dad was in the front chatting animatedly to the driver who wore a peaked cap and sat to attention with his hands, clad in black leather gloves, casually resting on the steering wheel.

'I'd better go in with Robbie and Alfie,' stated Mum and I watched as she billowed through the graveyard, long skirts flowing and bracelets jangling, holding on tight to Robbie's skinny young arm as Alfie, on his lead, trotted obediently beside them. I watched them as they joined all our friends in the dark hole of the church doorway. I could see Maggie and Stephen, Kath and Paul hurrying away from a gravestone that was nestled in a corner, hidden away like a secret, overhung by a beautiful pink blossom tree. There was Tom with his parents and his brother, Danny, and Rowan and Jane with Ash and Willow, and Will and Liz. Then there were all the girls from the salon, Kayleigh from the sanctuary and other family members, some of whom I hadn't seen for years. In fact some of them I hadn't seen since my first wedding. How on earth would they recognise me?

Even a few councillors had turned up, now that I was Councillor Laurel Masters (soon to be Garthwaite, of course) having been elected to a place on the council after Councillor Melrose won his well-deserved place with the district.

Becky's voice cut into my thoughts.

'Do you remember when you said our family was depleted with only three, Mum? And you wanted to get a dog or a cat to make it right?'

Turning to her I said, 'Yes, I remember

saying that, ages ago . . . I felt that we needed someone else to make us complete, and then we got Alfie.'

'Yes,' she replied. 'Alfie made our little family complete — our little unit. But look at all the people standing outside the church — they're your friends, well . . . I mean . . . our friends, that want to be with you today to celebrate your wedding, which goes to show that we weren't depleted at all really, were we?'

I shook my head and smiled at her.

'No, we weren't. But I just couldn't see it then, could I?'

My thoughts turned to Jack and I wondered if he was there now inside the church, waiting for me, the ring that he kept checking with nervous fingers, safely in his pocket for he decided against a best man. He couldn't choose between Stephen and Paul, so decided to have Alfie as best dog instead. I can't wait to see him greeting me with Jack. After all, next to Jack, Becky and Robbie, I count Alfie as one of my dearest friends. Closing my eyes I indulged myself and pictured

Jack's tall, muscular frame clad in a dark suit, his hair neatly trimmed and the designer stubble that I so loved to touch covering his cheeks and his chin. I think of his eyes that glow like sapphires and his strawberry-red mouth. A delicious tremble shoots its way through my body and the urge to see him, to gaze in to his blue eyes, becomes overwhelming.

'Are you ready, Laurel?' asks Dad, turning around in the front seat to look at me. 'Or are you trying to be fashionably late?'

'Yeah, come on, Mum,' urged Becky, 'I want to get the aisle bit over with. I'm really nervous.'

'You?' butted in Dad, 'Nervous? What have you got to be nervous about? You're a right bobby dazzler, you are!'

There was a cool breeze that lifted the hem of my skirt as I stepped out of the car into the blinding light of the sun. Holding on to Dad's arm, Becky walking stately as a galleon beside us, my heels tip tapping on the stony path, I saw something from the corner of my eye. Was it a flash of light, or the ghost of a smile on a red painted mouth?

Confused and my heart beating fast, I saw a woman dressed in fashionable ripped black jeans and a summery white jacket standing beneath one of the stately yews that are scattered throughout the cemetery. She has short blonde hair and a painted face and her eyes are very blue surrounded by thick black lashes.

Paula? I thought and stiffened beneath Dad's grip until he said, 'Come on, Laurel, there's no need to be nervous. You're as bad as your beautiful bridesmaid here.'

It can't be her, I thought as we approached her slowly, slowly on our long walk through the cemetery to the massive wooden church doors. *She's in prison, she got a year, a whole year . . . it can't be her . . .*

We were almost abreast with her when, to my horror, the woman moved towards us.

Just when I thought she was going to open her mouth to speak to me, she lifted her arm and shouted, 'John! Over here . . . I'm over here...'

A man hurried over to her from somewhere behind us.

'I couldn't see you, Lois,' he said. 'I was waiting over there.' He pointed. 'And I was reading the grave stones . . . call me melancholy but, well it's so fascinating!'

Hooking her arm through his, they walked away together, talking and laughing, stopping again to pore over the gravestones, reading snippets to one another.

It isn't her, I thought with a sigh of relief. I could tell easily that it wasn't her now, just someone who looked a bit like her — someone called Lois who, like Paula, had short blonde hair and blazing blue eyes.

Was I looking for her in every young woman I saw? I must be, because she haunted me — she haunted me even in my dreams. I still pictured her running towards the animals' cages and smell the petrol as drops flew through the air from the red can that swung from her hand like a beacon in the darkness.

We ducked into the musty old church. It was cool and dim inside and, until my eyes adjusted, I could only see a vague outline of Dad and Becky. Only her bright blue dress and small posy of vibrant flowers shone through the gloom.

Dad squeezed my arm reassuringly and said, 'Well, this is it then, Laurel — take a deep breath. Becky, are you ready?'

I sensed a little nod of her head.

The organ swelled into the wedding march and, with butterflies fluttering madly in my tummy, I gripped Dad's arm. With Becky close behind, I took several big, bold steps which will take me to Jack.

★　★　★

Rasping breath followed me as I climbed the steep hill to Cobby Cairn. The muscles in the backs of my legs almost screamed with pain as step after step I drew closer and closer to the top.

Alfie streaked past as, with one more

deep breath, I gave it my all and ran the few final steps to the top, my fingers stretching out taut and white as, at last, they find the reassuring stones of the trig point.

I bent at the waist, feet wide, breathing deeply as my heart rate slowed and I stayed that way, head hanging, until I heard the thunder of someone's feet and more rasping breathing.

Glancing up, I saw fingers touch the stones exactly where mine had just been, fingers that were just as white and taut as mine were, and whoever it was gave a huge sigh of relief.

'Good God, Laurel,' said Jack, barely able to speak and panting hard. 'Why didn't you tell me how hard it is to be a runner?'

'Did I ever tell you it would be easy, Jack?' I asked.

'Well no, not in so many words, you just made it look that way.' He grinned, his handsome face flushed and his teeth showing very white. My eyes travelled his body, looking just as muscular and fit as I knew it would in short shorts and a vest top. For it was a cloudless summer day with a sky as blue as Jack's eyes and a hot sun that was making even Alfie sweat.

'Wow,' he said, 'I can see why you like coming up here, Laurel, the view is magnificent.'

He stood looking out over the vista, his hands on his hips and his chest still moving up and down with his rasping breath.

'Yes, it's amazing up here. And I know it's hard for a first run, but it's worth it.'

We gazed out at the view, particularly beautiful on such a lovely summer day.

'Do you know,' he said, thoughtfully, 'I think the only time I've been up here was when Alfie found the puppies, and both of you were trying to keep them warm, and you were singing a song about bones. And I drove up that time.'

I giggled and said, 'Yes, it was just there in that bush . . . Alfie always goes to have a look. He's sniffing there now.' Having recovered my breath I sang, '*Dem bones, dem bones, dem dry bones, now shake those skeleton bones ...'*

Jack laughed as we watched Alfie, his long nose deep in the bushes, sniffing and snuffling like a pig searching for truffles. We smiled at each other and Jack sank to the ground, leaning back gratefully against the trig as if it was a pillow.

I followed suit and sat down beside him taking a deep draught from a bottle of water that I carried in a belt around my waist.

'The next time you run with me, I'll take you on the route over the glen towards Skelly. OK?'

'Is that further than today's run?'

'Yes ... but flatter!'

'Ah ... that's good then. Isn't it?'

Nodding, I say, 'It's a cinch.'

Closing my eyes I turn my face up towards the sun feeling the warm rays on my face, only slightly worried that the wrinkles around my eyes would be burnt deeper into my skin. After all, what did it matter really? The wrinkles that fanned out around Jack's eyes when he smiled looked incredibly sexy. Maybe I could cultivate mine to look the same.

He reached out and took my hand.

'Do you know, Laurel,' he said lazily, his thumb making tiny circles on my palm and the inside of my wrist which was making me feel soft and gooey as wax. 'You never did give me my marks out of ten . . . you know, after that trial period.'

'Are you still going on about that?'

He nodded. 'Of course.'

Alfie wandered over and I poured out some water for him into his collapsible travel bowl. After slurping it messily he turned around and around in circles a few times, sniffing at the ground. Then he lay down and, curling into a ball, closed his eyes.

'OK then,' I said. 'Four out of ten!'

'Only four? That's an insult!' he said in mock anger.

Leaning closer and enfolding me into his arms, his face and lips very close to mine, he said, 'I think I can change your mind.'

'Oh really?'

'Yes, I think I can get a higher score . . .'

'Oh yes?'

He smelled warm, of sunshine and salty sweat. His lips just above mine hovered for a moment, teasing me, a smile tugging at their corners, until they touched mine very lightly, as light as the touch of a feather, and then with more urgency and more urgency still. After a while he broke away and I slumped back, exhausted and my lips tingling, against the rough stones of the trig point.

'Well?' he said as I lay with my eyes closed, soaking up the sunshine, my heart pounding so it could be seen fluttering like a bird beneath my breasts.

'Laurel?'

'Ten,' I told him breathlessly, 'That was definitely worth a ten.' With a smile I thought back to a few months ago when everything seemed to be over between us and I wasn't willing to give him a score at all.

'Yes!' he crowed, punching the air,

'Would you like more of that later? Because there's more, lots more.'

'Yes, please,' I said. 'I can see that you're going to make me a very happy woman.'

Holding out his hand he pulled me up and crushed me to him, my body slotting in to his as if we were indeed meant to be.

'What you said to Robbie on our wedding day,' I whispered in his ear, 'Did you really mean it?'

'Yes, I did, Laurel, one hundred per cent!'

I put my face up to his and he kissed me, again, his lips very soft and very warm.

'He was clever, wasn't he? Making the connection between the sanctuary and puppy love?'

I nodded and smiled as we clambered to our feet and began the descent back down the long track to the canal, our trainers sliding on the dry earth, little puffs of dust around our feet. Alfie sprang ahead, happy and excited, his tongue lolling from his mouth.

Jack held tightly to my hand until we were on the tow path and we could run beside each other again, dodging in and out of the tow path traffic of ducks and geese and swans.

A couple of nasty geese stuck out their long necks and hissed at us as we ran past, and a gentle breeze blew blossom from the trees. It put me in mind of the confetti swirling around us, glinting in the sunshine like silver sixpences, as we stood outside the church amongst the tumbledown gravestones on our wedding day. Husband and wife at last.

I conjured up the day again, and the faces of all our friends, happy to be with us to celebrate, sprinkling the confetti that floated in the air, coating our hair and our clothes like glinting jewels, until landing gently on the ground like drops of rain falling from the sky.

'Is it your turn next, Dad?' asked Robbie with a grin, nudging Ash and Willow who stood watching in awe.

Will and Liz smiled at each other, Liz

blushing a hot red as if she were indeed the bride already.

'Hey, guess what, Mum,' said Robbie, smiling all over his cheeky face.

'What Robbie?' I asked him patiently. 'You and Jack . . .'

'Mr Hollywood,' stage whispered Becky into his ear, with a smile and a wink at Jack.

'What about me and Jack?' I asked him. 'Well . . . it's not just a puppy love, is it?'

Everybody exploded into laughter. Jack, eyes narrowed, assessing him, said, 'Oh yes, and what do you know about puppy love then, Robbie?'

Robbie hesitated, everyone waiting for what he would come out with next, before saying, 'Well, at first I thought it was just for puppies. But it's for people too, isn't it?'

There was general laughter again and Jack bent down slightly to Robbie's height.

'Oh yes, Robbie, puppy love is definitely for people and not for puppies.

And sometimes it's thought of as a shallow kind of love . . . a first love that might not last forever. I hope that one day you meet someone and can share a real love like me and your mum. So, no, what we have is definitely not just puppy love.'

'Wow,' I said, as Jack pulled me into his muscular arms and, blue eyes blazing with passion, gazed at me for a moment or two before his lovely mouth finally met mine.